"You have some nerve,"

Valentina stormed as Josh pulled her into the center of the room. "What makes you think I want to dance with you?"

"I know you don't," Josh said calmly. "But we have to keep up appearances. I'm the groom's best friend. How would it look if you and I ignored each other?"

"You're the friend from hell," she said soberly, gazing up at his handsome face.

"How can you say that?"

"Perhaps because you're trying to prevent my marriage."

He gathered her closer to his lithe body. "I'd prefer to say I'm trying to prevent you from making a mistake."

But Valentina knew her biggest mistake was letting Josh hold her so close....

Dear Reader,

Celebration 1000! continues in May with more wonderful books by authors you've loved for years and so many of your new favorites!

Starting with . . . *The Best Is Yet To Be* by Tracy Sinclair. Bride-to-be Valentina Richardson finally meets Mr. Right. Too bad he's her fiancé's best friend!

Favorite author Marie Ferrarella brings us BABY'S CHOICE—an exciting new series where matchmaking babies bring their unsuspecting parents together!

The FABULOUS FATHERS continue with Derek Wolfe, a *Miracle Dad*. A fanciful and fun-filled romance from Toni Collins.

This month we're very pleased to present our *debut* author, Carolyn Zane, with her first book, *The Wife Next Door*. In this charming, madcap romance, neighbors David Barclay and Lauren Wills find that make-believe marriage can lead to the real thing!

Carol Grace brings us a romantic contest of wills in the *The Lady Wore Spurs*. And don't miss *Race to the Altar* by Patricia Thayer.

In June and July, look for more exciting Celebration 1000! books by Debbie Macomber, Elizabeth August, Annette Broadrick and Laurie Paige. We've planned this event for you, our wonderful readers. So, stake out your favorite easy chair and get ready to fall in love all over again with Silhouette Romance.

Happy reading!

Anne Canadeo
Senior Editor
Silhouette Romance

Please address questions and book requests to:
Reader Service
U.S.: P.O. Box 1325, Buffalo, NY 14269
Canadian: P.O. Box 1050, Niagara Falls, Ont. L2E 7G7

Tracy Sinclair

THE BEST IS YET TO BE

Silhouette
ROMANCE™
Published by Silhouette Books
America's Publisher of Contemporary Romance

 SILHOUETTE BOOKS

ISBN 0-373-19006-9

THE BEST IS YET TO BE

Copyright © 1994 by Tracy Sinclair

This edition published by arrangement with Harlequin Enterprises B.V.

® and TM are trademarks of Harlequin Enterprises B.V., used under
license. Trademarks indicated with ® are registered in the United States
Patent and Trademark Office, the Canadian Trade Marks Office and in
other countries.

Printed in U.S.A.

TRACY SINCLAIR,

author of more than forty Silhouette novels, also contributes to various magazines and newspapers. An extensive traveler and a dedicated volunteer worker, this California resident has accumulated countless fascinating experiences, settings and acquaintances to draw on in plotting her romances.

A Note from the Author

Dear Reader,

I was so pleased to have my book, *The Best Is Yet To Be*, included in Celebration 1000! I wrote my very first romance for Silhouette, and now, almost fifty books later, I still can't wait to start a new one.

My characters become very real to me. I share all their experiences. Sometimes when I visit a place I've written about, I expect to see the palazzo my hero owned in Venice, or the castle I dreamed up in Spain. I only hope I have succeeded in making these people and places come alive for you, too.

I want to thank all of you who wrote to tell me you enjoyed my books. I sincerely hope I can continue to please you.

Yours truly,

Tracy Sinclair

Chapter One

The engagement of Valentina Richardson and Warren Powell was reported in newspapers all across the country. Society editors salivated at the prospect of a lavish VIP wedding, while gossip columnists were more interested in the fact that Warren was a billionaire. They didn't actually accuse Valentina of being a fortune hunter, but the implication was there. Why else would a young, beautiful woman marry a man twice her age?

Valentina's family reacted with disbelief. Her sister, Toni, was the first to telephone. "Is it true? Are you really going to marry Warren Powell?"

"I wanted to tell you myself, but the media got hold of the news and went on a feeding frenzy. It's been awful! They all think I'm marrying Warren for his money." Valentina's deep blue eyes were shadowed.

Toni hesitated. "He *is* old enough to be your father."

Valentina's slender body tensed. "Is that all anybody can think about? Warren is a wonderful man! I've never met anyone so intellectually stimulating. He's also a thoroughly nice person. I never thought I'd be lucky enough to meet a man like him."

"So you do love him." Toni's relief was evident over the phone.

"I'm not sure I know what love is," Valentina answered slowly. "I thought I was in love once, and you know what happened."

"I realize it was a devastating experience, but you can't dwell on the past. I just don't want you to make another mistake."

"I'm not," Valentina said confidently. "Warren is a dear man. We expect to have a happy life together."

"Have you really given it enough thought?" Toni asked hesitantly. "You're twenty-seven and he must be close to sixty."

"Don't exaggerate. He's only fifty-six—in the prime of life, actually. People only think of Warren as being old because he's a legend in the electronics industry. When my publisher suggested I write a book about him, I wasn't sure anybody would be interested. I was afraid he'd be one of those brilliant computer nerds who speak a different language from the rest of us. But Warren isn't like that. He's warm and kind and funny."

"If you're really sure, I wish you all the luck in the world." A tinge of doubt still colored Toni's voice.

"Thanks, but I already have it."

Valentina truly believed that. Her marriage to Warren Powell might not be a grand love affair, but she liked and respected him, and he felt the same about her. Those were the important things in a relationship—friendship and mutual compatibility. Passion only clouded a person's judgment. She was living proof of that!

Contrary to what everyone believed, Warren's money had nothing to do with Valentina's decision. She even turned down his first proposal. They'd grown close during the weeks they'd worked together, but the idea of marriage had never entered her mind. Warren still talked about his adored wife who'd died a year before, after a marriage that had lasted almost thirty years.

He didn't pretend that he expected this marriage to be the same. Warren was very open with her. "I realize I'm twice your age, but I think we could make a go of it. I'm not exactly over the hill yet, and there are compensations. I can give you everything you've ever wanted," he'd told Valentina.

"That would appeal to a lot of women, I suppose, but I would never consider marrying for money," she'd answered evenly. "I'm flattered by your offer, but I'll have to refuse."

"I'm sorry if I offended you. I didn't mean it to sound like a business proposition. I'm very fond of you, and I believe we could have a good life together. If you don't find me totally repulsive, that is." He'd smiled appealingly.

"You know I don't, and the age factor doesn't bother me."

"What is it, then? We seem to be quite well suited—unless there's somebody else."

When she told him there wasn't, he asked her to think it over.

Valentina thought about nothing else for several days. She knew what had prompted his proposal. Warren was lonely; he didn't want to grow old alone. But neither did she. The prospect had bothered her occasionally, since she'd renounced all thoughts of marriage after the fiasco with Robert. How could she ever trust another man? Yet she trusted Warren. That was the deciding factor, along with all his other good qualities.

Joshua Derringer would have found that hard to believe. His first reaction after reading the announcement in the newspaper was outrage. His normally generous mouth was compressed as he reached for the telephone.

"I suppose you heard about Valentina and me." Warren sighed. "You and everybody else in town. My phone's been ringing off the hook."

"Why didn't you tell me you were considering something like this?" Josh's handsome face was grim.

"I wasn't aware that I needed anyone's permission." Warren's voice was deceptively mild.

Josh was reminded of how the older man's gray eyes could freeze. Warren looked like a genial college professor, but it was folly to underestimate his intelligence or challenge his authority. He hadn't gotten where he was by being soft.

Josh modified his tone. "I was just surprised, that's all. You never mentioned that you were thinking of getting married again—certainly not to someone like Valentina. What I mean is, you've only known her a short time," he added hurriedly.

"At my age you don't have all the time in the world," Warren said wryly. "It wouldn't matter, though. I know everything about her I need to know. She's brought the sunshine back into my life."

"I know it's been lonely since Marian died. I should have spent more time with you."

Warren chuckled. "We play poker every Tuesday night, and you drop by on the weekend. I'm already cutting into your love life. A handsome young fellow like you could be out every night with a different beautiful woman. You should be glad Valentina's taking me off your hands."

"I've been there because I wanted to be. You're the best friend I've ever had," Josh said soberly. "I wouldn't be where I am today if it weren't for all the help you gave me when I was starting my own company."

"Yes, you would. It might have taken a little longer, but you'd have made it because you're bright and you're tough. You're like a son to me, Josh, and that's why I want you to be happy for Valentina and me. You'll see what a fine person she is when you get to know her."

Josh had an instant mental picture of Valentina. She was undeniably beautiful. A slender but provocative figure, long tawny hair that was a blend of light brown with golden highlights, thickly fringed, deep blue eyes, widely spaced in a heart-shaped face.

It wasn't difficult to see what had attracted Warren. Josh had felt a jolt of electricity himself, the first time he'd seen her. She'd been coolly polite, however, subtly rebuffing any advances before he even made them.

Josh had known more than his share of acquiescent women, so he wasn't insecure. He accepted the fact that

Valentina wasn't attracted to him, but her unfriendliness was puzzling. Now he understood. She was after bigger game.

"I just want you to be happy," he told the older man helplessly.

"I appreciate your concern, but you don't have to worry about me. Valentina made me realize my life isn't over."

"I could have told you that."

Warren laughed. "No offense, but it's more convincing when it comes from a pretty woman."

"She's certainly that, all right." Josh's tone wasn't as warm as the compliment.

Warren was too astute not to notice. "I know what people think—there's no fool like an old fool. That's probably the kindest thing they're saying. Public opinion doesn't bother me, but I'd like to think my friends trust my judgment."

"We're always here for you." That was the best Josh could manage.

"Just promise you'll reserve judgment until you really get to know Valentina."

"I intend to give it top priority."

Josh's eyes were narrowed and his sensuous mouth was compressed in a straight line as he replaced the receiver. "She's not going to get away with this," he muttered. "Warren might have fallen for her act, but she hasn't won yet."

Valentina was as upbeat as Warren about their coming marriage. The only thing that marred her happiness was the press. They phoned at all hours of the day and night, asking outrageous questions. How did it feel to be engaged to one of the richest men in the country? Had she signed a premarital agreement giving up any claim to his fortune? Did they plan to have children?

At first she tried to be polite, or at least civil. But when a reporter for one of the tabloids asked if Warren had settled a lump sum on her, and if so, how much, she hung up on him. That didn't discourage them. They hung around her house, stuck cameras and microphones in her face and even went through her trash.

When she turned into the driveway of Warren's estate in Portola Valley, sixty miles from San Francisco, two men were lurking around the gate. One of them approached the car while the other turned on a video camera.

"When's the wedding going to take place, Miss Richardson?"

She was trapped in her car waiting for the electric gates to open, so she said, "We haven't set a date yet."

"Where are you going on your honeymoon?"

"We haven't talked about it."

"How do you feel about having stepchildren older than you are?"

Valentina gave him an outraged look and drove through the gate, swerving around the photographer who tried to block her path.

Warren's two grown children were another source of glee to the press. It would be only a matter of time until they found out his son and daughter were adamantly opposed to the marriage, even though Warren had assured them their inheritance wasn't in jeopardy. His children had never brought him much joy.

Helen was married to a marketing analyst and lived in Scarsdale, New York. She had a generous trust fund from her mother, which she used as a club to keep her ineffectual husband in line.

Gary was as weak as his sister was strong. He was twenty-eight years old, but had never "found himself." He was presently taking graduate courses in ancient Far Eastern religions at U.C. Berkeley. The campus was located across the bay from San Francisco, but he never came to visit his father or even phoned, except to ask for money. Warren had virtually no contact with his children.

Valentina was still steaming at the insolent questions as she parked her car and went into the house. Warren's private secretary was passing through the hall.

"There ought to be a law against reporters harassing people," Valentina muttered, although she didn't expect sympathy from the older woman.

Florence Haney had been hostile from the moment Valentina had started working with Warren. At first Valentina thought the woman was afraid the book would turn out to be one of those warts-and-all biographies. That would account for her attitude. Florence was fiercely loyal after ten years in Warren's employ. But over the ensuing weeks, Valentina came to realize the real reason for her animosity. Florence was secretly in love with her boss.

Warren pooh-poohed the idea when she mentioned it to him. "She still calls me Mr. Powell after all these years. Florence was closer to my wife than she's ever been to me. She was wonderful to Marian during her illness."

Valentina didn't doubt that. From all accounts, Marian Powell had been a charming woman. But after she was gone, Florence must have hoped her secret dreams about Warren might come true.

She was about forty-five now, Valentina guessed, terrifically efficient, but nondescript. Florence could have been an attractive woman, with a becoming hairdo, a little makeup and stylish clothes. She had a nice figure, but it wasn't noticeable under the severe business suits she always wore.

Valentina understood the other woman's frustration, but she wished Florence would lighten up. Her hostility made working conditions difficult, since they had to see each other every day.

During his wife's long illness, Warren had moved his office to a wing of the large house so he could be closer to her. After Marian's death he simply stayed there. With fax machines and modems, it was just as efficient and eliminated commuting to Silicon Valley.

"Don't talk to *me* about reporters!" As expected, Florence wasn't receptive to Valentina's complaint. "They call here at all hours of the day and night. We can't get any work done."

"I'm sure they'll lose interest soon." At least Valentina hoped so.

"Nothing like this would ever have happened when Marian was alive," Florence muttered. She walked away without waiting for a reply.

Valentina sighed and went to look for Warren.

He glanced up from his desk and smiled at her. "You look a little frazzled. Was the traffic heavy?"

"About usual. An accident on the Sand Hill exit had cars backed up for miles. I sound like one of those people who give traffic reports on the news." She laughed.

"That long drive every day must be grueling. I can't see why you don't simply stay here. There's certainly plenty of room."

"Wouldn't the gossip columnists just love that?"

"You've stayed overnight occasionally when we worked late."

"That was before we were engaged. Now every move we make is scrutinized."

Warren shrugged. "You worry too much."

"I'm not the only one. Florence is livid over the publicity."

"It will die down."

"That's what I told her. I just don't understand it," Valentina said plaintively. "It isn't as if we were rock stars or anything like that. Naturally our engagement would be reported—you're a prominent person—but why this Roman circus? You're not the first man who ever married a younger woman."

"I suppose it's because I've always been fairly reclusive. I never could understand people who liked to see their name splashed all over the newspapers."

"You must really hate all this publicity." Valentina looked at him soberly.

"It's worse for you." His jaw set grimly. "Some of the things they're printing are despicable. I'm tempted to sue, but that would only give their lies wider coverage."

"I don't care what strangers think. I just wonder how your friends feel about us."

"If they're true friends, they're happy for me."

"Not necessarily. They have your best interests at heart. I can see why they'd be concerned."

"My judgment has been pretty sound so far," Warren answered dryly. "I'm still CEO of a company that pioneered the electronics field."

"I wasn't suggesting they thought you were senile—just caught in the wiles of a designing woman." Valentina grinned. "Be honest. Haven't some of your friends urged caution?"

He looked uncomfortable. "They don't know you like I do."

"I was right! You *have* been warned."

"I'm sure people are curious about you," he replied evasively. "I'm afraid I've been selfish about keeping you all to myself. It's time that changed. Perhaps it might be a good idea to have an engagement party, so everybody can meet you and see how lovely you are."

"I don't imagine they're interested in my appearance," she said wryly.

Warren smiled. "The men certainly will be. They'll all wish they were in my shoes. Let's pick a date, and then we'll make up a guest list."

Valentina dreaded the thought of being on display in front of a lot of people who had already formed an opinion of her—probably an unfavorable one. Before she could frame her objections tactfully, Warren's assistant joined them.

Chuck Kowalski was a tall, lanky young man with sandy hair and a pleasant face. He was usually smiling and unflappable, but today he looked perturbed.

"I'm sorry to be late, Chief," he apologized.

"Relax, you don't have to punch a time clock," Warren said mildly.

"I know, but I have a lot of work to do on the SX-2 project. Jenkins is almost ready to complete the circuitry."

"Have you been able to bypass the scanners?" Warren asked.

"I think we've got it licked. His report is supposed to be on my desk this morning. I expected to get on it first thing, but Denise's car wouldn't start. I had to drive her to her aerobics class." Chuck looked embarrassed. "She gets leg cramps if she misses her exercises."

"I admire her dedication. I could use more exercise myself."

Warren was being charitable, since his opinion of Chuck's wife was tepid, at best. Valentina had never met her, but she'd heard that Denise was a demanding woman who treated Chuck abominably. He didn't seem to be aware of it. In his eyes, she could do no wrong.

"Well, I'd better get to work," he said. "I just wanted to tell you I was here. I'll be in my office if you need me."

"He's such a nice fellow," Valentina said after Chuck had left.

Warren nodded. "And a brilliant computer engineer. He's developing a system that will prove invaluable to the business industry. I've put him in complete charge of the project."

"You wouldn't think his wife's aerobics class would take precedence."

"They say love is blind, and Chuck is living proof," Warren said ironically.

"I've never met Denise. What is there about her that's so special?"

"You'll meet her at our engagement party."

"I'm not sure I want to."

"You should never leap to conclusions about people. They aren't always what they seem. You might like her."

"I doubt it. I don't approve of the way she makes Chuck jump through hoops."

"Since he doesn't object, it's nobody else's business." Warren dismissed the subject. "Get a pad and pencil. We need to start making up a guest list for the party."

"I'm running way behind schedule on the book. We'd better do some work first."

"This won't take long."

"You never know when we'll be interrupted. We really should take advantage of the moment," she insisted.

He looked at her with a slight frown. "Do I detect a case of cold feet?"

"Only about the party," she confessed. "What if your friends don't like me?"

"Then we'll make new friends," he said jokingly, before turning serious. "When they get to know you, everyone will love you the way I do."

"I hope so," Valentina answered soberly. "I'm sure some of them will try to talk you out of it right up until our wedding day."

"Maybe this will show them how committed I am." Warren reached into his pocket and brought out a square velvet box. "I intended to give you this tonight over a romantic, candlelit dinner, but I think you need some convincing right now." He handed her the box.

Inside was a ring, set with a large emerald surrounded by glittering diamonds. Valentina's eyes widened. "Oh, Warren, it's magnificent!"

"You mentioned once that you liked emeralds, but if you'd prefer a diamond I'll exchange it."

"I love it!" She went over to throw her arms around his neck.

"I hoped you would." He pulled her onto his lap and slipped the ring on her finger. "Now we're officially engaged."

"We didn't need this," she said softly.

"I know, but it tells the world we're not merely having an affair," he teased.

"You're a true gentleman." Valentina laughed, hugging him tightly.

"Shall I turn around and tiptoe out?" Josh was standing in the doorway, gazing at them sardonically.

"It's too late now. You've spoiled the mood." Warren chuckled. "Come on in. What brings you here at this time of day?"

"I thought we could have lunch together."

Warren glanced at his watch as Valentina self-consciously got up from his lap. "It's a little early for lunch."

"We can take a swim first," Josh suggested.

"Don't you work anymore?" Warren asked.

"That's the pleasure of owning your own company," Josh said easily.

"Don't hand me that," Warren scoffed. "You work harder than any of your employees."

"You've shown me the error of my ways," Josh drawled. "If I ease up a little, I, too, might find a beautiful bride."

"You'd break too many hearts." Warren turned to Valentina. "This young buck has a little black book that Errol Flynn would have envied."

"Somehow that doesn't surprise me," she answered sweetly.

"Warren is prone to exaggeration. He's also fooled by appearances on occasion." Josh's smile didn't reach his eyes.

"I've often thought the same thing," Valentina said evenly.

Warren's face was expressionless as he looked from one to the other. "If you're through discussing me, why don't we all go out by the pool and have a Bloody Mary?"

"You two go ahead," Valentina said. "I have to transcribe my notes."

"We haven't done any taping yet," Warren pointed out.

"I meant, I have to organize my material," she corrected herself hastily.

"I'm sure it can wait. I want you and Josh to get to know each other better. You're my two favorite people." Without waiting for a reply, he pushed a button on the intercom. "I'll be out by the pool, Florence. Tell Connie to bring us three Bloody Marys and set another place for lunch. Josh will be joining us."

"I have those evaluation reports for you to look over," his secretary replied in a disapproving voice.

"I'll get to them after lunch."

Valentina reluctantly accompanied the men outside, since she couldn't get out of it gracefully. Josh was the epitome of everything she disliked in a man—from his super good looks to his confident manner. Women were only trophies to him. Warren was so astute in every other way. How could he admire a man like that?

They were seated at an umbrella table when Consuela brought their drinks. She and her husband, Jose, had worked for Warren for years, like most of his employees.

"No munchies, Connie?" Warren smiled at the woman.

"I don't want you to spoil your lunch," she answered with an equal mix of familiarity and respect. "We're having chiles rellenos."

"Nobody makes them like you do," Josh said. "I hope there's enough for me."

"For you, always," she answered fondly.

Valentina looked on sourly as the housekeeper fell for his pseudo charm. What a phony he was!

Warren raised his glass. "To friendship."

Josh lifted his own glass. "And to vanquishing one's enemies."

"Don't you have something to add?" Warren asked Valentina.

"Here's to recognizing the difference between the two," she said in a brittle voice.

"You're too young to have enemies," Josh remarked smoothly. "How old are you?"

"That isn't a question you ask a lady," Warren chided.

"It is when she's as young as Valentina. Then it's a compliment."

"You must not read the newspapers," she said. "My age has been reported endlessly."

"But not very much more," Josh said blandly. "Are you a native San Franciscan?"

"No." She didn't embellish her reply.

"Valentina lived in New York before she moved here," Warren said.

"Wonderful city. I have a lot of friends there," Josh remarked. "Perhaps we have mutual acquaintances."

"I doubt it. New York is a big city."

"Were you born there?" he persisted.

After an imperceptible hesitation, she said, "Yes."

"Does your family still live there?"

"Are you moonlighting as a reporter?" she asked lightly. "I get these questions thrown at me night and day."

"They've been harassing her terribly." Warren frowned. "I wish there was some way I could put a stop to it."

"I'm sure Valentina can tough it out," Josh said dryly.

"You've got that right." She looked at him directly.

Before he could answer, Consuela came to announce lunch was served.

There were five of them around the dining room table. Florence had been included during Marian's illness, and Chuck usually joined them if he was in the office at lunchtime. Valentina always welcomed his presence, since he offset the older woman's taciturnity. Meals were awkward otherwise.

Warren glanced around the table with satisfaction. "This is an unexpected pleasure, having you all here. It's like a party."

"A brief one for me, I'm afraid," Chuck said. "I hope you won't mind if I eat and run. I have a lot of work to do."

Josh regarded him with interest. "I hear through the grapevine that you're coming out with something really hot."

"Rumors are always flying around," Chuck said dismissively. "Don't believe everything you hear."

Warren glanced at him with a raised eyebrow. "I scarcely think my best friend is going to rip us off. What you heard is true," he told Josh. "Once we get the bugs out of this program it should be a bonanza."

"The rich really do get richer." Josh grinned. His merriment faded as he glanced at Valentina. "You'll have a full-time job spending Warren's money."

Her eyes sparkled dangerously, but she didn't allow anger to color her voice. "What else would people have to talk about if I didn't?"

"It looks like Warren already raided his piggy bank." Chuck was staring at Valentina's hand. "I hope Denise never sees that ring. She loves jewelry."

"What woman doesn't?" Valentina smiled.

"Marian never cared much for it," Florence said unexpectedly. It was the first time she'd spoken, and everyone looked at her in surprise, almost as if they'd forgotten she was there.

Warren broke the moment of silence. "Everyone has different likes and dislikes."

"I only wish Denise liked the simpler things in life." Chuck sighed. "My finances are already stretched like a rubber band."

"Is that your subtle way of hitting me up for a raise?" Warren asked, smiling.

"It wasn't my intention, but I wouldn't turn it down if you're in a generous mood." Chuck grinned.

"This is your best shot at it," Josh drawled. "While he's walking around with his head in the clouds."

It wasn't a relaxing lunch. Chuck was the only one who seemed unaware of the undercurrents swirling around. Soon after he left, the luncheon party broke up.

Valentina breathed a sigh of relief as she followed the two men out of the dining room. She was taken by surprise when Josh turned suddenly and started back into the room.

They collided and she was thrown off balance. His arms reached out instinctively to steady her. For a moment that seemed to last an eternity, she was cradled against his hard frame.

Valentina's heart started to beat rapidly as she became aware of the taut muscles in his lithe body and the solidity of his broad shoulders and chest. Every inch of him was unmistakably male.

Josh was the first to react. "I'm sorry. Did I hurt you?"

"No, I . . . it's all right."

"I almost forgot to thank Connie for a terrific lunch."

"Yes, it was good, wasn't it?" she murmured.

Valentina was shaken by her physical reaction to a man she didn't even *like*. Josh was a superb specimen of manhood, though, there was no denying that.

"I have to get back to work," Warren said. "Florence will start to nag if I don't look over those evaluation reports."

"I can take a hint." Josh laughed. "I'll leave as soon as I pop in on Connie."

"Stay as long as you like. Why don't you and Valentina go for a swim?" Warren left without waiting for an answer.

Something flickered in Josh's eyes as they wandered over her body. "Seeing you in a bathing suit would be almost too much good fortune for one man."

"You have an amazing faculty for making even a compliment sound like an insult," she replied angrily.

"Why would I want to insult you?"

"We both know the answer to that—you think I'm a fortune hunter. Well, who gave you the right to sit in judgment? Maybe you should take a long look at *yourself*. I don't think a womanizer is any more acceptable."

"What makes you think I'm a womanizer?"

"I know your kind. Women are just trophies to you."

"You must have known the wrong kind of men."

"Are there any other kind?" she asked scornfully.

He looked at her curiously. "Is that why you're going to marry Warren? Because a younger man gave you a bad time once?"

"I thought you'd made up your mind that I'm marrying him for his money."

Josh ignored the comment, continuing to stare at her. "There will always be a few bad apples in the barrel, but you can't let an unfortunate experience spoil your life."

"I haven't. You might not believe it, but Warren and I are completely compatible."

"How about love? I didn't hear any mention of that. When he holds you in his arms, do you enter a different world? Or are you just compatible there, too?"

Valentina's cheeks turned scarlet. "We don't...I mean...'
She stumbled to a halt.

Josh looked at her incredulously. "I can't believe what I'm hearing. If you were promised to me I'd want to keep you in bed for a week. I'd kiss every inch of your beautiful body until you begged me to make love to you over and over again."

"You mustn't talk like that," she murmured, averting her face.

Josh's erotic words aroused feelings she'd thought were safely buried. His sensuous voice made her body throb with an urgency she was sure he could satisfy with mind-spinning expertise.

"You're right. Warren is my friend." Josh's jaw set grimly. "That's why I intend to do my damnedest to stop you from marrying him."

"Why are you so sure I won't make him happy?" she asked in frustration.

"Because you're marrying him for the wrong reason. Either you really are a fortune hunter or you're a coward."

"I don't have to stay here and listen to this," she said icily, turning away.

He gripped her arm and pulled her so close she could see the spiky black lashes fringing his hazel eyes. They glowed like the green-and-gold eyes of a stalking panther.

"Did I come too close for comfort?" Josh asked softly. "Is Warren the father figure that will protect you from all the hot-blooded young men you can't deal with?"

"You don't know what you're talking about," she whispered.

He smiled sensuously. "Then why is your mouth trembling?" He traced the shape of her lower lip. "How long has it been since you were kissed passionately?"

She broke away like a startled deer, composing herself with an effort. "I won't tell Warren about this conversation—for his sake, not yours. But from now on you'd better stay away from me. I can fight as dirty as you can, and in this case I'll win. Whether you like it or not, I'm going to marry him."

Josh stared at Valentina's stiff back as she stalked away. "We'll see," he muttered.

Chapter Two

Valentina did her best to talk Warren out of the engagement party, but for once he remained firm. As the guest list grew, she became more dismayed.

"Is there anybody you *don't* know? We seem to have the entire population of San Francisco on the list, even a lot of city officials. This isn't a party, it's an extravaganza!"

"No point in leaving anyone out and having hurt feelings."

"We won't even get around to greeting all these people."

"Sure we will, although there won't be time for lengthy conversations. That's one of the bonuses." Warren smiled. "We don't get stuck with a lot of bores. Politicians can take an hour just to tell you how happy they are to see you."

"I've never planned a party of this magnitude," Valentina said helplessly. "I don't know who to seat with whom or what to serve. Not to mention flowers and music and all the other details."

"Relax, honey. Florence will take care of everything. All you need to do is go shopping and buy yourself a beautiful gown. Shoot the works, and send the bill to me."

"Not until after we're married," Valentina said firmly. "I can afford to buy my own dress."

Warren smoothed her hair lovingly. "I wish those reporters could hear that."

"They probably wouldn't believe it," she said grimly.

Valentina spent a lot of time picking out a dress for the party. With regret she passed up a scarlet-and-white strapless number that was spectacular and also rejected a gold lace sheath that was becoming on her but too sexy. This had to be a very special gown—glamorous yet elegant and tasteful.

She finally settled on a black organza that bared one shoulder. It was spangled all over with silver stars and tiny sequins. Multiple petticoats, layered under a long skirt banded by silver cord, made the hem billow out like a bell.

On the night of the party Warren held her arms out from her sides and gazed at her admiringly. Valentina's long tawny hair was caught up and secured at the crown of her head, leaving little tendrils curling around her face and at the nape of her neck.

"You look exquisite," he said. "Everyone will wonder how I persuaded you to marry me."

She glanced at the sparkling emerald on her finger. "I think they've already decided that."

The party was held in the ballroom of a nearby hotel. It soon filled with chicly dressed women, and men in dinner jackets. Valentina had invited a few of her own friends, but the majority of the guests were strangers to her.

Warren stayed by her side during the early part of the evening, introducing her to everyone. They were all pleasant and offered congratulations, but Valentina could see the speculation in their eyes. The women put her through an inspection worthy of an X-ray machine.

It was a relief to see Chuck in the crowd. He was the only one, so far, who didn't either resent her or suspect her motives. Chuck was a thoroughly nice person.

"This is quite a turnout," he remarked. "I'll bet you didn't get many refusals."

"No, everybody wanted to see the scheming adventuress who trapped the poor, befuddled billionaire."

"Nobody could make the mistake of underestimating Warren that badly, and I'm sure they just wanted to meet you."

"What planet have *you* been living on?"

"There are always some small-minded people," he conceded. "But why worry about them? You and Warren are happy, that's the important thing. Anybody who has trouble with that can go take a flying leap."

Before she could express her appreciation for his support, they were joined by a beautiful blond woman. She was very glamorous and had a really sexy figure. Her low-cut, beaded sheath revealed curves in all the right places.

Chuck's smile lit up his entire face. "This is my wife, Denise. You've heard me talk about her."

"You're his favorite topic of conversation," Valentina smilingly told the other woman. "It's so nice to finally meet you."

"I've heard a lot about you, too." Denise's avid gaze scanned Valentina's dress and hairdo. Her eyes widened when they zeroed in on the emerald ring. "Is that your engagement ring?" She reached for Valentina's hand. "It's gorgeous!"

Chuck groaned. "I knew it was going to cost me when she got a glimpse of that."

Denise's sulky mouth turned down at the corners. "You couldn't afford anything like this if you worked for the next fifty years."

Valentina was appalled. How could she denigrate her husband that way, and in front of a virtual stranger? "I don't think you can put a price tag on sentiment," she said evenly.

"I notice you didn't ask Warren to take it back and buy you a smaller one," Denise drawled.

"I can't compete with the boss, but I can promise you a surprise on our anniversary," Chuck told her.

"How long have you been married?" Valentina asked, thinking it best to change the subject.

"It will be two years," the other woman replied.

"Denise gave up her career to marry me," Chuck said proudly.

"Really? What did you do?" Valentina asked her.

He answered instead. "She was a starlet at Universal Studios in Los Angeles."

"How exciting. What movies were you in? Maybe I saw some of them."

Denise laughed shortly. "You'd have had to look fast. I only had a few walk-ons."

"You would have been a star if you'd stuck with it," Chuck said confidently. "A talent scout spotted her at a beauty pageant," he told Valentina. "Denise was Miss Georgia Peach."

"She isn't interested in my life story," his wife said, although she didn't look displeased.

"I never would have guessed you were from the South," Valentina commented. "You don't have the slightest trace of a Southern accent."

"I used to have a really thick one, but after the studio signs you, they turn you over to a speech coach. They also provide acting classes and lessons in makeup. You get the full treatment at first." Denise's eyes were bitter. "They promise to make you a star, and then one day you wake up and realize it was just a lot of hot air."

"I imagine it's a tough business," Valentina observed.

"For a woman, it is. When you're nineteen you've got the world by the tail, and you think big things are going to happen. You don't realize you'd better score fast. By the time you get into your middle twenties you're over the hill. *You* know how important youth is to old men."

Valentina's teeth clicked together. "If you're referring to Warren, I don't consider him an old man."

"She didn't mean it that way," Chuck said hurriedly. "Denise thinks Warren is terrific."

"Did I hear my name mentioned?" Warren joined them. "Is everyone having a good time?"

"It's a wonderful party," Denise cooed, her discontented expression vanishing. "We're so pleased to be invited."

"What would a party be without my right-hand man? And his wife," Warren added belatedly.

"I just know Valentina and I are going to be great friends," Denise gushed. "We have so much in common. If there's anything I can do to help with the wedding, I hope you'll call me," she told her.

"I'll keep it in mind," Valentina answered neutrally.

"If you'll excuse us, there are some people I want Valentina to meet," Warren said.

When they were out of earshot, she said, "Thanks for rescuing me. What a terrible woman!"

"She's not a very happy person," he admitted. "I've often wondered why she married Chuck. He doesn't seem to be her type."

"I can give you the answer. Denise's face and figure are her entire stock in trade," Valentina said succinctly. "She was getting older and men weren't showering her with proposals. He wouldn't have been her first choice, but maybe she got the impression that he had a bright future."

"He does. Chuck is still young, but I'm grooming him for bigger things."

"I only hope he doesn't burn himself out trying to satisfy her. He'd do anything to make her happy."

A gray-haired man approached them. "I haven't met your lovely bride-to-be yet."

After Warren had made the introduction, they exchanged pleasantries for a few moments. Then the man switched his attention to Warren.

"I noticed your stock jumped two points last week. Would this have anything to do with the very hush-hush project you're supposed to be working on?"

"You know how erratic the stock market is," Warren answered evasively. "Even the weather is more predictable."

"You're saying you *aren't* coming out with a new program?"

Warren smiled. "Would I tell the competition if I were?"

"It must be pretty hot if you're playing it this close to the vest."

"I hate to say it, but you gentlemen are getting old." Josh had joined their little group. "How can you talk business when you're with the most beautiful woman in the room?"

Valentina avoided looking at him, but in one brief glimpse she'd noticed how his snowy linen shirt accentuated his deep tan.

"You're perfectly right," Warren agreed. "It was inexcusable."

"I'll try to make it up to her. May I have this dance?" Josh asked her.

"No, thank you," she answered coolly. "I find the conversation fascinating."

"She's not only beautiful, she's tactful." Warren laughed. "Go ahead, my dear. I want you to enjoy yourself."

Josh took Valentina's hand and led her away before she could object. Although, what could she say in front of Warren? When they were alone, she wasn't as constrained with Josh.

"You have a great deal of nerve," she stormed. "What makes you think I want to dance with you?"

"I know you don't," he said calmly. "But we have to keep up appearances. I'm Warren's best friend. How would it look if you and I ignored each other?"

Her chin set stubbornly. "I don't care how it looks."

"Do you want a rumor to start circulating that you're trying to alienate Warren from his friends?" Josh asked softly as he took her in his arms on the dance floor.

"You're the friend from hell," she said soberly, gazing up at his handsome face.

Josh was the epitome of sophistication in his elegantly tailored dinner jacket and pearl studs, but that was misleading. Underneath that civilized exterior was a hard-as-nails street fighter. Valentina didn't trust him for a minute.

"How can you say that?" he asked smoothly.

"Perhaps because you're trying to prevent my marriage."

He gathered her closer to his lithe body. "I'd prefer to say I'm trying to prevent you from making a mistake."

"As though you cared about *me*," she scoffed.

"I could, very easily," he murmured.

Valentina tried to put distance between their bodies. His was too blatantly masculine. "If you plan to try seduction, I'll save you the trouble. It won't work."

Josh laughed unexpectedly. "Well, it was worth a try."

She felt an inexplicable twinge of regret that it was just a maneuver on his part. What was wrong with her? This man was her mortal enemy!

"Don't you find me even a little bit attractive?" he teased. "I have a lot of good qualities once you get to know me. I'm a dutiful son, a hard worker and a loyal friend."

"How loyal is it to try to seduce your best friend's fiancée?"

"How honorable is it to marry someone you don't love?" he countered.

"Love means different things to different people."

"Possibly. But it universally includes a physical relationship. Platonic love is another term for friendship."

"I didn't say our feelings for each other were platonic," she said carefully.

"I'm glad to hear that, for Warren's sake," Josh answered dryly.

"You'd never understand, so I don't know why I'm even bothering," Valentina said angrily. "To you, love is a wild, passionate affair for a brief period, then on to the next encounter. That isn't love, it's sex!"

"You say the word with such disgust. Sex can be a beautiful act between a man and a woman who care about each other."

Her mouth curved sardonically. "For a couple of hours, anyway."

"I don't know where you got the idea that I'm some kind of modern Don Juan who indulges in one-night stands solely to boost my ego."

"Why else would Warren mention your little black book with such respect?"

"It was a joke!" Josh's frown turned into an impish smile. "Nowadays men use a Rolodex."

She gave him an outraged look. "Isn't modern technology grand? I suppose you even have automatic dialing."

"It saves energy for the more important things." His eyes glinted mischievously.

"Spare me the details," she said coldly. "I'm supremely uninterested in your love life."

"You were the one who brought it up."

"Not intentionally, I assure you."

"I'm crushed. I thought you were finally finding me intriguing," he teased.

"Only as an adversary—one that's more bothersome than troubling. Even *you* should realize you're fighting a losing battle. Look at all these people here tonight for our engagement party. I'm sure some of them don't approve of me, but they've accepted the fact. Why can't you?"

Josh's bantering manner vanished. "Losing a skirmish isn't like losing the war. You aren't married yet."

Valentina was shaken by his ruthless expression. Even his taut body was menacing. She moved back instinctively, but his arms tightened around her. As a tiny chill rippled up her spine, a couple paused beside them.

"You two look so serious," the woman said archly. "Does Warren know you're making out with his fiancée?"

Josh's face reverted to its former charm. "Actually we were discussing the wedding."

"Warren is a lucky man," the woman's partner told Valentina gallantly.

"Thank you. It's nice to know his friends are happy for us." She lifted her chin and looked directly into Josh's eyes.

He held her gaze. "Warren's happiness is very important to his friends."

"When is the wedding?" the woman asked.

"We haven't set a date yet," Valentina answered. "I'd like to finish my book first."

"It's so romantic the way you met. What made you decide to write a book about Warren?"

Josh smiled sardonically. "How many billionaires are there in the country?"

"Actually it was my publisher's idea," Valentina said evenly, refusing to react. "I wasn't sold on the project at first, but he talked me into it."

"It's just like kismet," the woman cooed. "You were destined to meet."

"Warren didn't have a chance," Josh drawled.

"Well, we certainly wish you both a lot of happiness."

Valentina waited until the couple had moved away. "Why didn't you just make up a placard and picket outside the ballroom?"

"I prefer a more subtle approach." He smiled.

"Like acting as if you're attracted to me?"

"That doesn't take acting ability. You're an amazingly beautiful woman." His fingertips trailed over her bare shoulder. "It would be easy for any man to lose his head over you."

"Or pretend to. I'm going back to Warren." She pulled away and started off the dance floor.

Josh followed her. "All right, if you must. We'll just have to finish our conversation another time."

"Don't count on it!"

"It's something I'm looking forward to." He took her hand and held on when she would have withdrawn it. "Face it, sweet Valentina, you and I are engaged in all-out war, and I haven't wheeled out my big guns yet."

The ripple of apprehension she felt was merely due to Josh's dynamic personality, Valentina assured herself. He gave the impression of being invincible. But what could he actually do to her? There was only one thing in her life she was ashamed of, and that was safely buried in the past.

Valentina vowed to avoid Josh from then on, even if it meant being rude. Her resolution was unnecessary, however. He didn't come near her for the rest of the night. She spotted him in the crowd occasionally, dancing with a different woman each time and dispensing his facile charm. All of his partners were starry-eyed.

Valentina breathed a sigh of relief when the evening finally wound to a close. Even though Josh had given up actively harassing her, she'd been constantly braced for the unexpected.

When she and Warren were waiting for his car to be brought around after the last guest had departed, he put his arm around her shoulders. "I'd say the party was a success, wouldn't you?"

"I'm sure they'll talk about it for days." She smiled.

"You were the hit of the evening, my dear. Everyone told me how lovely you are. Josh certainly thought so."

Valentina's smile vanished. "That doesn't count for much. He never met a female he didn't like."

Warren looked at her with a slight frown. "I thought tonight had changed your mind about him. You two spent a lot of time together."

"*You* were the one who told him to dance with me."

"I wanted you to enjoy yourself. It wasn't much fun standing around listening to two stodgy old men talk business."

"You aren't old *or* stodgy. I would have preferred listening to your conversation."

"Josh must be losing his touch."

Their car pulled up and Warren helped Valentina inside. He walked around to the driver's side without giving her a chance to vent her annoyance.

When they pulled away she said, "I'll never understand why men admire studs so much."

"I wouldn't put Josh in that category," Warren protested.

"You just implied that he scored with every woman he set his sights on. What would *you* call him?"

"As I understand it, a stud is a man who's interested solely in sex, without any regard for his partners. Only the numbers count. Josh doesn't fit that profile. Women are attracted to him, and vice versa, but he's certainly not indiscriminate or uncaring."

"At least that's what you'd like to believe," she said mockingly.

Warren turned his head to stare at her. "Do you honestly dislike him that much?"

"I don't really know him," she answered carefully.

"Exactly. I don't understand your antipathy. Did he say something insulting to you? I can't imagine Josh doing such a thing, but if he did, I want to know about it."

Valentina realized she'd been too candid about her feelings. Creating a rift between the two men would make Warren unhappy and cause the kind of gossip Josh had warned her about.

"I have nothing against him personally," she said hurriedly. "I guess I'm just suspicious of any man who feels he has to charm every woman he meets."

"He can accomplish that without even trying." Warren smiled. "Maybe the charm thing is automatic, but Josh is one of the most honorable men I know."

With other men, Valentina thought cynically, but she didn't voice her opinion.

Warren sensed her reservations. "If he's broken some hearts along the way, I can assure you it wasn't deliberate. I can say that truthfully, after observing his relationships through the years."

"How long have you know Josh?"

"It must be ten years or more. Someone sent him to me for advice when he was first starting his own business. Josh was in his twenties at the time." Warren smiled reminiscently. "He reminded me of myself at that age—cocksure of his own ability. I knew he was a winner after talking to him for fifteen minutes. Today Josh has one of the largest software companies in the industry."

"But he still comes to you for advice."

Warren shook his head. "He doesn't need it anymore. We talk business occasionally, since it's a common interest between us, but that isn't our primary purpose in getting together. We simply enjoy each other's company, in spite of the age difference. That's why I hoped you two would be friends."

"I'll try." She managed a smile. "I certainly wouldn't want to break up a long-standing friendship."

"You'll like him when you really get to know him. Josh is coming over for brunch tomorrow. We'll all have a nice, relaxing day together."

Valentina's nerves tightened instantly. "Why don't I leave you two alone? I'm really beat after the party and all the preparations for it. I planned to sleep late and lounge around my apartment all day."

"You can do that by the pool."

"It's such a long drive back and forth."

"I don't know why you didn't spend the weekend at my house," he said impatiently. "Who cares what a bunch of reporters print in their yellow journals?"

"They give such a nasty innuendo to everything. The less they have to write about, the better."

"They'll just make up things," he said with a sigh. "But all right, I understand. I'll pick you up tomorrow and Josh will take you home. That way you won't have to make the long drive alone."

"No! I mean, that's such a lot of bother. It will be much more restful for everybody if I just stay home and loaf all day. That's what I really feel like doing."

Warren glanced over at her. "Let's be honest with each other, Val. I've always felt very close to Josh. He's the kind of man I wish my son could have been. But I wouldn't dream of forcing him on you. I don't want to cause you a moment's unhappiness."

Her throat felt tight. "Dear Warren, you're almost too good to be true."

He reached over and took her hand. "I care about you, my dear."

"I feel the same way about you," she said softly. "What time would you like me to come over tomorrow?"

"I thought we just settled that. Stay home and relax. It would be awkward to put Josh off at the last minute, but you don't have to worry about this happening again."

"You're making a big deal out of nothing," she said deprecatingly. "I have a bad habit of making snap judgments about people, and that's what I obviously did with Josh. If you feel this strongly about him, I must be wrong."

"I honestly think you are, but you're entitled to your opinion." Warren pulled up in front of her apartment house and prepared to get out. "Rest up tomorrow, and I'll see you on Monday."

Valentina was powerfully tempted to let it go at that, but she had to see Josh sooner or later—unless she was willing to let Warren give up a treasured friendship for her. How could she be that selfish?

"I'll be over tomorrow about noon," she said brightly. "No more arguments. You've made me see Josh in an entirely different light, and I want to take a second look."

Warren and Josh were lounging around the pool in swimming trunks when Valentina arrived the next day. Warren was still trim for his age, with only a slight thickening around the waist. He was in excellent condition, but even in his prime he probably never had Josh's magnificent physique. Few men did.

Josh's long body was relaxed on a chaise, his muscular legs crossed at the ankles. Even in repose there was a leashed vitality about him, like a superb jungle animal that could spring to life in an instant.

In a brief glance Valentina noticed his deep tan and the curling dark hair on his broad chest. It tapered down in a V before disappearing inside the white bathing trunks that hugged his lean hips like a second skin.

Warren stood and came over to kiss her. "I feel guilty for asking you to make that long drive, but I'm glad you're here. What would you like to drink? Can I fix you a mimosa? That's what we're having."

She grimaced slightly. "I had enough champagne last night."

"This has orange juice in it." Josh held up his glass. "That makes it nutritious."

"I still think I'll pass. I didn't have any breakfast this morning, and I don't want to drink on an empty stomach."

"Are you afraid you'll say something too revealing?" Josh drawled.

Valentina forced herself to smile at him. "No, I'm afraid I'll fall asleep. Drinking in the afternoon has that effect on me."

He looked slightly surprised that she hadn't snapped back at him.

Before he could try again, Warren said, "Connie left some platters of cold cuts and salads in the refrigerator. I'll bring lunch out, unless you'd rather go for a swim first."

"I forgot to bring my suit." Actually she had decided against it. Josh made her uncomfortable enough when she was fully clothed.

"No problem," Warren said. "Didn't you leave a suit here last week?"

"That's an old one I meant to throw out," she answered dismissively. "It doesn't matter. I don't feel like swimming, anyway."

Warren eyed her gray silk pants and long-sleeved pink-and-gray blouse. "Even so, you'd better put it on. You'll be too warm, sitting around in that outfit, lovely as it is."

"That was my main reason in coming today," Josh said. "To see you in a bathing suit."

"You're not missing much," she replied pleasantly.

His eyes narrowed as he stared at her, trying to assess this new tactic, but once again Warren intervened. "You don't really expect him to believe that, do you?"

"It doesn't matter. He was only being polite. If everybody's hungry, I'll go get our lunch."

"I'll do it. I didn't invite you here to work," Warren said.

"Connie did all the work. Stay here and talk to Josh. I'll be back in a few minutes."

Valentina was glad to get away, if only for a short time. Josh evidently intended to bait her all afternoon. It would take supreme self-control to keep from answering in kind. She opened the refrigerator, sighing deeply.

After taking the plastic wrap off a platter of sliced meat and cheese, a bowl of pasta salad and a tray of fresh fruit, she placed the food on a rolling tea cart and added a pitcher of iced tea. As she was filling a basket with bread and rolls, Josh came into the kitchen.

Valentina didn't let her instant tension show. "Lunch is almost ready. You can take that bowl of olives outside to munch on while I finish up in here."

Josh leaned against the kitchen counter instead, folding his arms across his chest while he gazed at her with a lifted eyebrow. "Would you like to tell me what game you're playing? I'm a little confused."

"I can't believe that," she answered mockingly. "You're so good at playing games."

"Ah, that's better. For a moment I thought you were a replacement for the real Valentina."

"You don't know the real Valentina," she said curtly.

"I know she's a fighter. Why this sudden turnaround?"

"There's just no pleasing you." Her eyes sparkled angrily. "If you want a sparring partner, go to a gym."

He smiled lazily. "I'm starting to enjoy our little skirmishes."

"Tell me something I *don't* know!" She banged the basket of bread down on the tea cart.

"All that sweetness and light out there was obviously an act you're putting on for Warren. Did he tell you to make nice?"

"For your information, he told me I didn't have to spend any more time with you if I didn't want to."

"But you're so charmed by my sterling qualities that you declined his offer," Josh remarked mockingly.

She gritted her teeth. "You already know what I think of you. But for some reason I'll never fathom, Warren values your friendship. If I let him see how I really feel, it will destroy your relationship. I don't want to cause him any unhappiness, so I'm going to be civil to you if it kills me— which is very possible."

Josh stared at her searchingly. "You'd really put yourself through that?"

"I have no choice."

"Until after you're married," he answered cynically.

She gave him a disgusted look. "That's about what I'd expect from you. I just wish Warren could see what you're really like. But since he has this gigantic blind spot where you're concerned, I guess I'm stuck with you for the rest of my life. Don't underestimate Warren, though. If you're too openly obnoxious to me, you just might outsmart yourself. He's quite fond of me, even if you can't understand it."

"That doesn't surprise me in the slightest." Josh's voice deepened. "You'd be very easy to love."

"I liked you better when we're enemies. Let's keep it that way," she said coldly, pushing the tea cart toward the door.

* * *

"I was about to send a search party." Warren looked up and smiled. "You two have a tendency to disappear on me. Are you trying to steal my fiancée, Josh?"

"If you weren't such a good friend, I'd certainly consider it." He gave Valentina a melting look.

"It wouldn't do you any good," she said lightly. "I've already made my choice."

Lunch was surprisingly pleasant. Although Valentina stayed on guard, Josh didn't toss any more barbs her way. It was all worth it when she saw how pleased Warren was that they were getting along.

They discussed last night's engagement party and some of the people who had been there. Then the conversation drifted to business.

"What do you think of Vantage Microscreen?" Josh asked Warren.

"They make a good product, but the company is badly mismanaged. I heard a rumor that they're headed for Chapter Eleven."

"You heard right. I made an offer to buy them out."

Warren frowned. "Do you think that's wise?"

"You just said they make a good product. Their problem is in the front office. The company is run by a bunch of incompetents. I'm sure I can turn it around and make it profitable."

"Perhaps in time, but in this down-turned economy it's wise to keep a large cash reserve. I don't like to see you overextend yourself."

"The time to buy is when the market is depressed."

"It's too volatile right now," Warren insisted. "The analysts are advising caution."

Josh grinned. "I've never played it safe. That's part of the excitement of life—living on the edge."

The older man shook his head. "Someday you're going to back yourself into a corner you can't get out of."

"I've always managed to land on my feet so far." Josh glanced over to where Valentina was lying on a chaise, listening to the two men with her eyes closed against the sun. "I think we put Valentina to sleep."

She opened her eyes. "No, I was just trying to learn something about the electronics industry."

"It's too nice a day to talk business." Josh rose and stretched, displaying impressive muscles. "Put your suit on and let's go swimming."

"You're supposed to wait for an hour after eating."

"That's an old wives' tale. Besides, it's been almost an hour." He forestalled her next objection. "Come on, I'll help you take the food inside and put it away."

Warren was no help. "The sun is really strong. You must be uncomfortable in that long-sleeved blouse," he told her. "Run along and change while Josh and I clean up."

They left her no choice. Valentina groaned inwardly, realizing she'd outsmarted herself. The bathing suit she'd left at home was a modest tank suit; the one here was a skimpy bikini.

Why did it bother her so much? she wondered, as she undressed in the cabana next to the pool. Because Josh made her feel like a sex object, she decided virtuously, denying her own physical attraction to him.

Chapter Three

Valentina's sapphire blue bikini was undeniably skimpy. It displayed the upper curves of her small, high breasts, a large expanse of slender midriff, and the long, graceful legs of a fashion model.

Josh and Warren both looked at her appreciatively, but Josh was also vocal in his admiration. "Would it be sexist if I said wow?"

"If you don't, I will." Warren smiled.

"Anyone would think you two had never seen a bikini before," she remarked lightly. "Are you going to sit there and ogle me, or are we going swimming?"

"Do I get my choice?" Josh's golden gaze traveled slowly over her graceful body, like a connoisseur regarding an art treasure.

Valentina turned away without answering and dived into the pool. When she surfaced, Josh was standing on the diving board. She watched him arch his body like an Olympic athlete and cut the water cleanly. Momentum propelled him half the length of the pool and he surfaced beside her, brushing the dark hair off his forehead. Their faces were so close she could see the droplets of water beading his black lashes.

"Nice dive, Josh," Warren called.

"I'll bet you can do better." Valentina swam over to the coping.

"Not even in my prime," Warren said.

"You *are* in your prime," she insisted.

"He just says things like that to get compliments," Josh joked. "We're on to you, Warren."

The older man joined them, and they all swam and played keep-away with a big rubber ball, amid much splashing and laughter. Finally Warren got out of the pool, declaring he'd had enough exercise. While Josh swam laps, Valentina floated lazily, closing her eyes and enjoying the sun.

"You look like a mermaid." Josh swam up to her with scarcely a ripple and combed his fingers through her long streaming hair.

Valentina was so startled that her head bobbed under the surface. She swallowed a mouthful of water and thrashed about, sputtering and choking.

Josh put an arm around her waist and thumped her on the back. "Hang on to me until you get your breath back."

She didn't have any choice, but even in the midst of a coughing spell, Valentina was conscious of Josh's nearly nude body. Her breasts were pressed against his hard chest, and their hips met and parted erotically as the buoyant water moved them back and forth. His shoulders felt cool and smooth under her circling arms.

Gradually, Josh's hand gentled, gliding over her back now. Unconsciously his head dipped toward hers. Their faces were very close. Valentina's eyes were riveted on his firm mouth. She parted her lips as their bodies swayed together and Josh's hand curved around her neck.

"Are you all right, Val?" Warren called.

For an instant, Josh's arm tightened around her. Then his taut body relaxed. "She's perfect," he answered, smiling at her.

Valentina returned to normal, her cheeks flaming at her own incomprehensible behavior. Pushing herself away from Josh, she swam over to the ladder and scrambled out of the pool.

"What happened?" Warren asked as he draped a large towel around her.

"I swallowed a mouthful of water. That will teach me to keep my mouth shut." She avoided looking at Josh, who had followed her.

"I'll bet it would be easier to give up swimming," he teased.

The telephone rang as Warren was about to come to her defense. His smile faded after a moment, and Valentina and Josh listened to his end of the conversation with concern.

"That's terrible!" Warren exclaimed. "Were they badly hurt? . . . Well, that's good news, at least. . . . Is there anything I can do? I want them to have the best care. . . . Yes, I'll get in touch with the doctor. Thank you for calling."

"What's wrong?" Josh asked when he hung up.

"Martha and Jay Dandrich were in an automobile accident. They're the young couple in charge of the Inner-City Children's Foundation I established," Warren explained to Valentina.

"Are they all right?" Josh asked.

"More or less. Jay has a broken arm, and Martha was diagnosed with a concussion, but it could have been a lot worse. They'll both recover."

"That's good. From what you told me about them, they're nice kids."

"Yes, and very competent, which presents me with a problem." Warren frowned. "The annual Foundation camping trip is scheduled for next week. The children will be terribly disappointed if we have to call it off. It's the only chance most of them have to see grass and trees. But who can I get to take charge at the last minute like this?"

"How old are the children?" Valentina asked.

"Between ten and thirteen."

"Then I don't see what the problem is. Kids are pretty self-reliant at that age. You shouldn't have any trouble getting somebody to fill in."

"It isn't that easy. I need a couple who are experienced at handling youngsters."

"What's the big deal? All they have to do is supervise their activities. I remember when I went to camp. It was

great fun. We swam and played tennis during the day, and
at night we had sing-alongs and toasted marshmallows
around the campfire.''

"It isn't a good idea to give inner-city kids a pointed
stick," Josh said dryly.

"You're being ridiculous," Valentina said impatiently.

"I'm afraid Josh is right," Warren said. "These are disadvantaged youths. They haven't been taught to play by society's rules. They can get out of hand if someone with
experience doesn't keep them in line."

"All children try to test authority. We played tricks on our
counselors, too." Valentina smiled reminiscently.

"I don't think Warren is talking about short-sheeting the
beds," Josh said. "Inner-city kids aren't likely to be adept
at tennis or the backstroke, either. They're better at running numbers and scaling fences to get away from the law."

"We're talking about children," she protested.

"Unfortunately, those are their skills." Warren sighed.
"We can't make a huge impact in just a week, but at least
we can give them a taste of the better life. And hopefully
instill a resolve to go for it. Some of these young people have
great potential. It would be a shame to have to call off the
trip. I'm afraid they'll take it as one more broken promise.''

"Surely you could get somebody if you paid enough,"
Josh said.

Warren slanted a thoughtful glance at him. "Money can't
be the only incentive. It would have to be someone tough
but fair. An authority figure they could also look up to.
Perhaps somebody who's made a huge success in his own
business, but who can still outrun and outthink them."

"Whoa! Hold it right there!" Josh shook his head. "If
you're talking about me, I wasn't volunteering."

"I wouldn't expect you to," Warren said mildly. "It isn't
your problem, it's mine."

"I'd like to help you out, but I don't know anything
about kids."

"Didn't you coach a Little League team?"

"Well, yes," Josh answered reluctantly. "But that was
different. I wasn't solely responsible for them, and I didn't

 have to worry that they'd deck the umpire if they objected to a call."

"Surely you're not afraid of a bunch of little children?" Valentina asked.

"I don't notice you volunteering to play housemother to the girls."

"I would, but I have to work on my book."

He raised an eyebrow. "I suppose *I* don't have to work?"

"You own your own company. You can afford to take a week off. I can't."

"That's a pretty lame excuse. Why don't you just admit the thought of spending the night in a sleeping bag panics you?"

"It wouldn't appeal to the children, either," Warren said. "We want them to enjoy the outdoors, not be turned off by it. That's why we put them up in a rustic motel near the lake."

"What kind of a camping trip is that?" Josh asked disgustedly. "I suppose they order breakfast from room service?"

"The accommodations aren't that plush. We try to provide the best of both worlds—a comfortable place to sleep and outdoor activities. Breakfast is served in the dining room, but they do have cookouts on the beach or at the barbecue pits in the park."

"It's still not my idea of a camping trip," Josh said. "We used to really rough it—sleep on a hard cot, wash in cold water, the whole nitty-gritty experience."

"That's their everyday life," Warren answered quietly.

"The poor little kids," Valentina said. "It must be a treat to stay in a motel."

"That's part of what they look forward to, sleeping only two in a room. I hate to be the one to tell them the trip is off, but I guess I'll have to."

Josh sighed deeply. "Okay, I know when I'm licked. I'll ride herd on the little monsters—but only the boys. I wouldn't know how to handle the girls."

"I'll bet that's the first time you've ever said *that*," Valentina commented. To her annoyance, he agreed with her.

"I suppose that's true." He chuckled.

"I really appreciate your offer, Josh. Now all I have to do is find someone to supervise the girls," Warren said.

"How about Valentina?"

"This isn't exactly her field of expertise."

"Oh, I see. It's all right for me to give up the comforts of home, but the little princess would be traumatized for life if she had to stay at a second-rate motel."

"Be fair, Josh. It isn't only that. She's never been exposed to the seamier side of life."

"Good heavens, I never thought of that!" Josh exclaimed with mock chagrin. "She might hear a few four-letter words."

"If you two are through discussing me as if I weren't here, may I say something? I wasn't raised in a vacuum, contrary to what you both believe," Valentina said evenly. "I know all the words you do—maybe more. They don't shock me. I may not know any disadvantaged people personally, but I doubt that you do, either," she told Josh. "I'll bet I can relate to them better than you can."

"Is that a challenge?" he asked.

"No, merely a statement of fact. I'm a lot more accustomed to the simple life than you are. You'd be lost without your car phone, your fax machine and all the other gadgets in your push-button life."

"Those are tools I use in my business. I suppose *you* could live without your telephone-answering machine and call waiting."

"A lot easier than you could," she said.

"We'll see abut that. Are you willing to put your money where your mouth is? A week in the country, miles from the nearest hairdresser, shopping mall and gourmet restaurant?"

"Also miles away from the nearest Jacuzzi and fitness gym," Valentina reminded him. "You'll never last the week."

"What's the bet? We have to have a payoff."

She thought for a moment. "A hundred dollars?"

Josh waved that away. "It should be something more meaningful than money." He looked at her speculatively. "The loser has to serve the winner breakfast in bed for a week. I'd better buy you an alarm clock. I get up very early."

"That's a ridiculous bet! Pick something sensible."

"Afraid you'll lose?" he taunted.

"No way! It just happens I don't eat breakfast, so I'd lose even if I won."

"You might change your mind." A faint smile lurked around Josh's firm mouth. "I cook a mean breakfast."

It didn't take much imagination to guess who his satisfied customers were. Josh had perfected his technique on many a morning after.

"Why don't you let me decide what the penalty is," Warren intervened tactfully. In the heat of the argument they'd almost forgotten he was there. "The entire discussion is academic, because neither of you are quitters. In the event that one of you does throw in the towel, however, you'll have to answer to me. Is that satisfactory?"

Valentina nodded. "It is with me."

"I suppose so." Josh grinned. "She probably can't cook, anyway."

As Valentina opened her mouth in rebuttal, Warren said wryly, "I wonder if I'm making a mistake sending you two off together. I want the children to learn to get along with people, not have you teach them how to wage sophisticated warfare."

"Don't worry, we'll be on our best behavior," Valentina assured him.

"At least in front of the kids," Josh added wickedly.

The phone rang again before Warren could comment. He picked it up and listened for long minutes. "It's nice of you to say so, Denise," he remarked finally. After another interval he said, "She enjoyed meeting you, too. As a matter of fact, Valentina is sitting right here. Would you like to talk to her?" He held the phone out.

"I'll get you for this," Valentina muttered.

"I just told Warren how fabulous the party was," Denise said. "Chuck and I had such a marvelous time, but the best part was meeting you."

"You're very kind," Valentina murmured.

"I really mean it! It was such a relief to talk to someone my own age for a change. Most of the wives at these things are practically middle-aged. I don't have anything in common with them."

Denise was in her mid-thirties, at least seven or eight years older than Valentina, and they wouldn't have had anything in common at any age, Valentina thought.

"They all seemed quite pleasant," she said aloud.

"But so deadly dull! And the majority of them have absolutely no clothes sense. If I had their money I'd know what to do with it, believe you me."

"Well . . . people have different priorities."

"I can certainly tell what *yours* are. That gown you had on was to die for. I'd love to go shopping with you one day."

"I don't really have much time for shopping. I'm a working woman."

Denise uttered a little trill of laughter. "I'm sure Warren would give you a day off."

"I don't work for Warren."

"Then we'll just have to do it on a weekend. Or better yet, maybe the four of us can go out to dinner one night."

"That's a thought," Valentina said vaguely.

"Why don't we make a date right now. We're free anytime you are."

"Oh. Well, the thing is, I'm going out of town for a week."

"How exciting. Where are you going?"

"No place glamorous. Actually, I'm going camping."

After a slight pause Denise said, "You're joking, aren't you?"

"No, it's a project of Warren's. He sponsors a camping trip for underprivileged youngsters every year." Valentina's eyes took on a mischievous sparkle. "You know, I just had a wonderful idea. Why don't you come along? It will be a lot of fun—early-morning dips in the lake before cooking breakfast over a campfire, then off on a brisk five-mile hike in the woods. How does that sound?"

"Like being in the army. If you don't mind, I'll pass on this one. Give me a call when you come back and we'll get together."

After Valentina hung up, Josh said, "Were you out of your mind? Going camping with Denise ranks right up there with slamming your finger in a car door."

"I knew she wouldn't go. I was just trying to get rid of her. She was backing me into a corner. She wants us to have dinner together one night," Valentina told Warren.

"Why don't you raise Chuck's salary so his wife won't feel she has to suck up to the boss?" Josh joked.

"He'll get a handsome bonus once he perfects our new project," Warren replied.

"When will it be ready?"

"Soon, I hope."

"There are a lot of new products coming out in the fall. I hear ComTac is working on some interesting new software," Josh said. "Have you heard about it?"

While they talked business, Valentina's thoughts reverted to the camping trip. How had she let the two men talk her into such a thing? She had no doubt that each had manipulated her for his own purpose—and she'd fallen for it! At least Warren's motives were noble, but what diabolical scheme was Josh planning to discredit her?

Valentina's chin firmed. Whatever it was, he wouldn't get away with it. By the time the week was over he'd respect her as a worthy opponent, if nothing else.

Cloverdale Lake wasn't built up like other California resort areas. Tourists stayed at the Pine Tree Motel, or else they camped out. Daytime activities were plentiful. There was swimming and boating on the lake, and nature trails wound through the surrounding woods.

A public swimming pool and playground were recent additions, fought against bitterly by the locals. Their fear that the place would become inundated with tourists was unfounded, however, because there wasn't anything to do at night. The small town nearby had only one bar, a rather rundown restaurant and a theater that showed very old movies.

The girls were not impressed. Six of them were packed into Valentina's Range Rover, and the noise and complaints had been constant during the ride from San Francisco.

"Well, we made it," Valentina said brightly. She glanced briefly at a slip of paper. "Everybody look for Maple Street. That's where we turn off to get to the motel."

"You mean this is where we're going?" Meg Corrigan stared disbelievingly out the window. "There's nothing here. What are we supposed to do for fun?"

She was a skinny thirteen-year-old with a face that would have been pretty except for a permanently belligerent expression. Meg was the undisputed leader of the group. All the other girls concurred with her opinions. Or else.

"We have a lot of things planned," Valentina assured her.

"Yeah? Like what, watching the grass grow?"

"We could have stayed home and had more excitement." Sally Johnson was quick to side with her friend. The two were about the same age.

"You mean dodging cars and hanging out on the fire escape?" Valentina asked dryly.

"At least there's some action in the city," Meg grumbled.

"Why don't you try to keep an open mind? You just might enjoy yourself."

"I'll bet!" the young girl muttered.

Josh was already at the motel with his group when Valentina arrived with hers. The boys were milling around the lobby boisterously, while the manager watched them with a worried expression.

The tallest of the boys tired of the horseplay and approached Josh. "When are we going to get our rooms?" That wasn't exactly the way the question was phrased. He used a descriptive word not heard in polite society.

"Watch your language," Josh told him. "There are ladies present."

"You got to be kidding! What planet are *you* from, man?"

"Just knock it off, Gary."

"Or what? I suppose you're going to make me?"

"If necessary." Josh's voice was pleasant, but he pinned the boy with a steely gaze.

After a moment Gary's eyes shifted. "Big deal," he muttered, walking away with an attempt at nonchalance.

Josh turned to Valentina. "You look frazzled. Did the girls give you a bad time?"

"They didn't learn their manners from Emily Post," she answered wryly.

"They'll settle down once we get them into their rooms." Josh glanced at a sheet of paper and started assigning rooms. "Gary, you and Mark will be in 105. Tony and John will share 107."

As he went down the list, Meg said to Valentina, "That's one foxy dude. Is he your old man?"

"Don't get any ideas. Josh and I are simply...friends."

"Oh, sure!" The young girl gave him an admiring look. "I wouldn't mind being his friend. He could hang his jeans in my closet anytime."

Valentina barely kept her mouth from dropping open. "Don't you think he's a little old for you?"

"Get real," Meg said witheringly.

Getting them into their rooms was no easy task. A number of squabbles broke out over whose room was larger or who had a better view, although all the rooms were essentially alike.

When the arguments had finally been settled, Josh said to Valentina, "You look like you could use a drink. How about it?"

She glanced around the lobby. "I don't see a bar."

"There isn't one, but I came prepared. Come to my room. I have a bottle of scotch in my luggage."

"I just hope the girls don't see us," Valentina remarked as she accompanied him down the hall and into a corner room. "Meg has already decided we have a thing going."

He grinned. "I hope you didn't disillusion her."

"I tried, but she didn't believe me." Valentina sank down in a chair with a sigh. "These kids are really heartbreaking. They're old beyond their years."

"It happens when you grow up on the streets."

"I hope we can give them a good week, if nothing else. But they seem so hostile. How can we get through to them?"

"By showing them we're on their side. They don't give their trust automatically."

"You challenged that young boy and made him back down. Won't he hold it against you?"

"I doubt it. Strength is the one thing they respect. We can't let them run wild, but I hope by the end of the week they'll learn that teamwork beats going it alone."

"I don't know if I can teach Meg anything. The only thing she respects me for is my imaginary affair with you."

He chuckled. "Say the word and we can make it a reality."

"So much for your friendship with Warren," Valentina replied dryly.

Josh's mouth firmed. "You know how I feel about your relationship with him."

"I'm sorry I brought it up. Can't we strike a truce for one week?" she pleaded. "I really need a friend. Or if that's too much to ask, could you at least stop sniping at me? I can't take punishment from the kids *and* you."

His frown disappeared. "I couldn't punish you if I tried," he said in a deepened voice. "You were made for pleasure, not pain."

"Please don't, Josh. That's just another form of harassment, and I have enough troubles already."

"You worry too much, that's your main trouble," he soothed. "What can happen in a week?"

"I don't expect anything to happen—that's not the problem. I just want the children to have a good time."

He shrugged. "It's pretty much their choice. We can provide the tools, but we can't build the house for them."

"How can you be so hard?" Valentina protested.

"I'm a realist and you're a romantic."

"That's a switch. I thought you'd decided I was a cold-blooded opportunist."

He stared at her moodily. "I change my mind about you every five minutes."

"You were a lot happier when you were sure I was a complete monster," she said ironically.

"I didn't think that. We might not agree on certain points, but I discovered a long time ago that nobody is all bad or all good. Temptation can cloud even a strong person's judgment."

"Surely not yours." Her voice was mocking. "You would never let your heart rule your head."

"Is that a challenge?" he asked softly.

Tiny warning hairs prickled on the back of Valentina's neck. The last thing she wanted was to give Josh an excuse to come on to her. She'd already discovered, to her dismay, how vulnerable she was to him.

Rising to her feet, she set her unfinished drink on the dresser. "I have enough challenges with those kids out there. What are we going to do with them this afternoon?"

"How about a nice long hike in the woods? That should dampen their natural exuberance a little."

"It might also incite a riot. They don't seem to be charmed by nature."

"Nobody ever promised you a rose garden," Josh grinned.

"You act like you're enjoying this."

"I am. Where else could I get you all to myself for a week?" he asked in a silky voice.

"Just me and a dozen potential juvenile delinquents. Sounds like fun."

"I believe in making my own fun."

As he sauntered toward her, she moved quickly to the door. "You'll have to start without me. I'm going to unpack."

Meg was coming down the hall when Valentina emerged. The young girl gave them a knowing look. "Just friends, huh?"

"Don't get any ideas." Valentina tried to look unruffled. "Josh and I were simply discussing plans for the afternoon."

"You can tell it like it is," Meg said calmly. "In my neighborhood we call it a quickie."

Josh found it difficult to contain his amusement. "You're way off base, kid. If I ever make love to Valentina, it won't

be a quickie. Now, round up the others. Lunch will be
served in the dining room in fifteen minutes."

The same squabbling occurred over the seating arrangements, but eventually they were all assigned to two round
tables, three boys and three girls at each. Valentina and Josh
took charge of different tables.

Tanya, a dark-eyed ten-year-old, scanned the menu. "Can
we order anything we want?"

"Within reason," Josh said.

"What does that mean?" Meg asked suspiciously.

Gary's lip curled. "It means you get to eat what he tells
you to."

"Within reason means you can't choose only desserts,"
Josh said patiently.

"Can I have a steak?" Gary asked.

"Sure. I'd suggest the sirloin. It has more meat than the
T-bone."

"Hey, cool!" Gary looked surprised and pleased.

At Valentina's table, Laura said, "I want a shrimp cocktail." She was about twelve, with long stringy hair.

Sally gazed at her scornfully. "That's yuppie food."

"I don't care. I never had one."

"You never had octopus, either. You want that?"

Valentina stepped in to quell the budding argument. She
and Josh managed to guide the children toward a nourish-
ing lunch, even if the combinations were a little bizarre.
Laura had pizza with her shrimp cocktail and a hot fudge
sundae for dessert.

When Josh glanced over with a raised eyebrow, Valentina shrugged. "It covers all the main food groups," she
said.

They were getting along fairly amicably when a troop of
children their age was ushered into the dining room by a
young man and woman in crisp white cotton pants and jade
green polo shirts with a logo on the pocket reading Camp
Wildwood. The boys and girls were all dressed alike in clean
khaki shorts and green polo shirts like the counselors. Their
faces were scrubbed and their hair was neat.

"Get a load of the Ken and Barbie dolls," Gary sneered. "Well, there goes the neighborhood."

"Settle down," Josh said.

"They make me want to barf," Gary growled.

"Yeah, let's toss their butts out of here," Meg suggested. "This is our turf."

"Chill out, both of you," Josh ordered.

After seating their group without any problem, the young couple approached Josh and Valentina and introduced themselves as Judy White and Dennis Gordon.

"We're all from the peninsula," Dennis said. "Where do your children live?"

"In beautiful downtown San Francisco—the slum area," Gary snickered. "That's when we aren't in Juvie—you know what that is, don't you?"

As Josh gave him a quelling look, Valentina said hastily, "They're all from the city."

"Maybe you can give us some pointers on how to keep our group busy up here," Judy said. "We usually spend this week at the old Farnsdale estate in Atherton. It's ideally located for day trips to the children's symphony, the zoo and the Junior Museum. Unfortunately there was a fire in the west wing of the house and it's closed for repairs."

"I suppose we were lucky this place could accommodate us at the last minute," Dennis remarked dubiously. "Although I don't know how we're going to keep the children amused."

"The park has a swimming pool, and you can rent boats at the lake," Josh said.

"Most of them have pools in their backyards. That's no big treat. They might enjoy waterskiing though, if we can rent equipment. I never thought to tell them to bring their own."

"They'll get bored doing that every day." Judy's face brightened. "I have an idea. Why don't we stage a swim meet? Our camp against yours. Children love competitions. We can also have sailboat races around the lake."

"I'm afraid Valentina and I have already planned our agenda for the week," Josh said.

"Give us some ideas," Dennis said. "Judy and I are at a loss."

"Well, we—uh—we're going to take them on nature walks, and . . ." Josh sent Valentina a silent plea for help.

"And teach them handicrafts," she said, off the top of her head.

"Be still my beating heart!" Meg commented sarcastically.

"You'll still have plenty of time for that," Dennis said. "Children really enjoy a little healthy rivalry. We can give prizes and have an awards ceremony. It will be fun."

"What are the prizes?" Gary asked. "Another week in this dump?"

"That's if you win," Meg said. "The losers have to stay *two* weeks."

Dennis gave her a determined smile. "It isn't what we expected, either, but we'll just have to make the best of things. You'd like to take part in a little friendly competition, wouldn't you?"

"It would make my day," she answered with heavy irony.

Dennis's smile wavered, but he was undeterred. "At least it would give them something to do." He appealed to Josh and Valentina. "What do you say?"

"I'm sorry, but our kids have a different field of expertise," Josh said firmly.

"What does that mean?" Meg demanded. "Are you saying we couldn't clobber those little geeks?"

"Yeah, we could cream them," Gary declared. "Just pick the place. We're ready any time they want to rumble."

"Splendid! How about this afternoon at two?" Judy asked. "We'll meet at the swimming pool." With a little wave of her hand, she and Dennis went back to their own tables.

"Great!" Josh muttered. "We're off to a flying start. I presume you do know how to swim?" he asked Gary.

"Sure, my old man used to take me to the gym before he cut out on us."

"How about the rest of you?"

When they all nodded, although some tentatively, Valentina said, "Aren't you worrying needlessly? I think Judy is right. It should be fun."

"If you're into mayhem." Josh lowered his voice. "What do you think is going to happen when Camp Privilege over there makes our kids look foolish?"

"You don't know that will happen."

"They have private pools and swimming instructors. Our team will be lucky just to keep their heads above water."

"We can't back out now. That would show we didn't have any confidence in them. What are we going to do, Josh?"

"Lay in a supply of bandages," he answered sardonically.

Chapter Four

Josh's worst fears were realized at the swimming pool that afternoon, although problems arose even before the meet began.

When they'd finished lunch, he said, "Okay, I'll expect everybody suited up and ready to go by a quarter of two."

"I don't have a bathing suit," Tanya said.

"Me neither," Sally said. "How about you guys?"

"We can wear our skivvies, but you chicks got a problem." Gary leered. "This might not be such a drag after all."

"How many of you need bathing suits?" Valentina asked. When they all raised their hands, she said to Josh, "We'll have to make a quick trip into town."

The shopping excursion was something like spilling marbles on a bare floor. All the children scattered in different directions and started pawing through racks of clothing.

"Stop horsing around. We're here to buy bathing suits," Josh ordered, as the management reacted with alarm.

"I already found the one I want," Meg announced, holding up a very skimpy bikini.

"What are you gonna do, stuff the top with old socks?" Gary hooted.

"How'd you like me to give you a nose job?" She stuck her chin out pugnaciously.

Valentina intervened hastily. "Let's go into the dressing room and try some of these on. All of you come with me," she told the girls, filling her arms with suits more appropriate for their immature figures.

The girls insisted on trying on everything in their size and some things that weren't. Then, after making a choice, they changed their minds repeatedly.

Josh didn't have an easier time of it. The boys rejected everything as wimpy. They wanted to wear their underwear and have Josh give them the money he would have spent on bathing trunks.

A frazzled hour later they were back at the motel and the children had gone to their rooms to change.

"I'm going to make Warren pay for this," Valentina said wearily.

"Even *he* doesn't have that much money." Josh sighed.

The other team was already at the pool when they arrived.

"We thought you chickened out," Tiffany Van Allen said. She was a beautiful fourteen-year-old with a slim figure and a shining blond ponytail.

"In your dreams, Barbie," Meg snorted.

"My name is Tiffany."

"Whatever."

"Now that we're all here, we can get started." Judy looked very official with a whistle around her neck and a clipboard in her hands. "The younger girls will compete first. Is that agreeable?" Without waiting for an answer she said, "Ten- to twelve-year-olds line up."

Three of Valentina's girls joined an equal number from the other group. When Judy blew her whistle, the Camp Wildwood girls dived cleanly and struck out for the far end. After an uncertain moment the other three jumped in feet first and thrashed around wildly, making little progress.

Meg stood on the sidelines screaming at them. "Move it! Are you going to let those dorks show us up? You guys are pitiful!"

"You're supposed to cheer them on," Valentina said. "They're doing the best they can."

"An elephant with two legs could swim better than that," Meg said disgustedly.

"Don't knock it till you've tried it," Josh said. "You're up next."

"I guess our team takes all three places," Judy called cheerily, draping towels around her girls. "Better luck next time."

"I'd like to wipe that smug look off her face," Valentina muttered to Josh. "This isn't a fair competition, and she knows it."

"Unfortunately, I'm afraid it's going to get worse," he answered.

His fear was justified. The swim meet was a rout. Meg and the other two older girls were hopelessly outclassed, even though they made a better showing than the younger girls. But sheer determination was no match for years of practice.

"Very good, Tiffany!" Judy exclaimed as she helped the youngster out of the pool. "You, too, Allison and Buffy. I guess we made a clean sweep," she called to Valentina. "Too bad about that."

Valentina gave her a strained smile before wrapping Meg in a towel. The girl's eyes were red, and she was panting heavily from her effort.

"Nice try," Valentina said, brushing the wet hair out of Meg's eyes.

"Are you kidding? We stunk!"

"I wouldn't say that."

"We lost, didn't we?"

"It happens sometimes. The important thing is you gave it all you had."

"Get real." Meg twitched away from her and went to stand by herself under a tree.

Josh's youngsters met with the same fate as the girls. Gary, at least, was a contender, but the other boys barely made it to the finish line.

Dennis was as patronizingly gracious as Judy. "Too bad your team lost, but you really gave us a run for our money, pal."

"Who you calling pal?" Gary asked truculently.

Dennis laughed. "I guess your children have something to learn about good sportsmanship."

Josh clamped a firm hand on Gary's arm as the youngster started forward. "We could all use a refresher course now and then," he said evenly.

"Right. Well, we'll give you a chance to get even tomorrow. I checked and they don't have any sailboats for rent on the lake, so what do you say to a rematch? Same time, same place."

Josh hesitated imperceptibly. "That's rather unimaginative. Surely we can think of some other kind of competition."

"Like what?"

"I don't know exactly, but I'll give it some thought. We can discuss it at dinner."

"Fine. And if you decide you don't want to compete against us, that's all right, too. We'll understand."

"We're not backing out of anything. I'd just like a level playing field next time," Josh said grimly.

Josh called a meeting in his room before dinner, deciding the kids needed a pep talk. They straggled in reluctantly, in a rebellious mood.

"Man, this trip is a real drag," Gary grumbled. "I've had more fun getting mugged."

"Yeah, that goes for me, too," Mark said.

There were mutinous sounds of agreement from all the others, even the younger ones.

"I realize today was rather disappointing," Valentina began carefully. "But you were up against unfair odds. Why don't you just concentrate on enjoying the water next time?"

"If you make me get in the pool with that Tiffany again, I'm going to hold her head under water," Meg warned.

"And I'll fix Duane so he don't walk so good. What the hell kind of name is Duane, anyway?" Gary asked disgustedly.

Josh knew this was no time to correct his language. "Let's face it, we were overmatched. You have nothing to feel badly about. I take full responsibility for accepting their challenge against my better judgment."

"Big deal! Why didn't you two take them on?"

"That's an interesting idea," Valentina mused, gazing at Josh's powerful shoulders and muscular thighs, outlined by his skintight jeans. "It would be a more even matchup."

Meg's expression was skeptical. "*He* could take them easy, but you look like one of those beach babes who's afraid to get her hair wet."

"Appearances are deceiving," Valentina said crisply. "I was on the swimming team in college."

"All right!" Gary exclaimed. "We'll cream them, and I'll take bets. Those little wimps ought to have plenty of money to lose. This is shaping up a lot better."

"There won't be any betting," Josh stated.

"It doesn't matter. Just so long as we get some of our own back," Meg said with satisfaction. "Will you guys do it?"

As the other children chimed in eagerly, Josh said, "Let me talk it over with Valentina." He beckoned her to a corner of the room.

"It's an inspired idea," she said enthusiastically. "Judy and Dennis could scarcely turn down the challenge, and I know we could beat them."

"Probably, but what would that prove? It wouldn't give the kids back their self-respect."

"Well, sure it would. We're on their team."

"They'd still have to live with the fact that they lost badly. That's what's eating at them. The only way they'll feel good about themselves is if they do the winning."

"We both know that isn't possible."

"Not in the pool, but what if they were competing at something they're good at?"

"Are you suggesting a spelling bee made up of four-letter words?" Valentina asked wryly.

"Don't sell them short. They have other skills those country club kids would fail miserably at."

"Like what?"

Josh's eyes twinkled mischievously. "Like dodging the cops and shinnying over fences."

"I don't get it."

"Trust me. To paraphrase Gary, we're going to mop up the floor with those little wimps."

The youngsters were waiting for them expectantly. "Well, what's the verdict?" Meg asked.

"It's a tempting idea," Josh answered. "But if Valentina and I substituted for you, they might think the rest of you were chickening out."

Meg's chin jutted forward. "I'd like to hear them say it."

"It wouldn't matter whether they said it to your face. That's what they'd be thinking."

Mark's face was dismayed. "You mean we got to go through that whole stinking thing again?"

A chorus of dissents rang out. "No way!"

"Count me out."

"Forget it!"

Josh held up his hand. "I didn't say that. We'll give them the competition they want, but on our terms. Now listen up. This is what we're going to do."

Dennis came over to their table as soon as they filed into the dining room. "Can I tell my team the meet is on for tomorrow?"

"We've already had a swim meet," Josh said. "I thought a gymkhana might be a nice change of pace."

"I'm not sure I know what you mean," Dennis said warily.

"Competitive games—footraces, an obstacle course, climbing a pole. We can use the jungle gym in the park."

"I don't know if I can agree to that. The children could injure themselves."

"They could also drown in the pool, but if you don't want to compete against us, we'll understand." Josh threw his words back at him.

Dennis's face reddened. "Just name the time and place. We'll be there."

"Splendid. How about ten o'clock in the morning at the park?"

The four adults met and decided on an agenda for the games. First would come the footraces for all age groups. The older children would also navigate an obstacle course over the jungle gym and climb the pole supporting the swings. These activities would be timed with a stopwatch. All of the groups would participate in an improvised version of the discus throw—hurling a rock at a distant target.

"Piece of cake," Gary bragged. "Just pretend you're driving off dudes trying to take over your turf," he advised the others.

The Camp Wildwood children were dressed neatly in their khaki shorts and green polo shirts, while the inner-city kids were a motley crew in well-worn jeans and shabby T-shirts. The comparison didn't bother them, however. What they lacked in appearance, they more than made up for in confidence that was soon justified.

Tanya won the footrace easily, closely followed by her teammates. Melissa, a plump little girl from Camp Wildwood, finished far behind.

"It wasn't a fair race," she whined. "I had a pebble in my shoe."

"That's nothing compared to the lead in your pants," Meg hooted. "Face it, kid, you couldn't outrun my grandmother."

"We teach *our* children not to gloat," Judy said stiffly.

"We teach *ours* not to make excuses when they lose," Valentina replied. She turned to Meg, however, and whispered, "Cool it."

Valentina was a fierce competitor, but winning for her own sake had never been this important. She stood next to Josh, shouting words of encouragement.

During the obstacle course she slipped her arm around his waist and leaned against him. When Gary momentarily lost his footing, she gasped and tightened her grip until their hips were pressed closely together.

Josh's expression changed as he glanced down at her rapt face. For just an instant his lips brushed her temple, but she was unaware of it, completely absorbed in the contest.

The day was a complete reversal of the previous afternoon. As the inner-city kids won event after event, they became less insufferable. Meg was almost gracious to Tiffany.

"If you'd worn jeans instead of those fancy pants, kid, you might not have finished in the cellar."

By the last race of the day, the opposition was crushed. When Gary crossed the finish line first, Valentina threw her arms around Josh's neck.

"We did it! We're number one!" She kissed him triumphantly.

What started as a victory kiss developed into something else. Josh lifted her off the ground and swung her around exuberantly. But when he set her on her feet, he didn't release her, nor did she unclasp her arms.

Their lips clung and he urged her closer. For a timeless moment their bodies were molded together and nobody else existed. They were lost in their own private world. As Josh's hands moved over Valentina's back, Meg's voice shattered the idyll.

"Break it up, you guys. We're the ones who deserve the congratulations."

Valentina drew away from Josh without looking at him. Her heart was beating rapidly as she struggled for composure. "You kids were fantastic," she told Meg.

"You've got that right. What do we get for it?"

"How about a sense of satisfaction?" Josh asked.

"Thanks for nothing," she answered, but it was said jokingly.

"Will you settle for dinner in town and a movie?"

"You got yourself a deal."

They all walked back to the motel together to clean up from their strenuous day. Valentina was grateful for the children's high-spirited chatter because it saved her from having to contribute to the conversation. She was still shaken from the heated moment in Josh's arms. It had been totally spontaneous, but that didn't make it any less reprehensible. She had responded to him wholeheartedly.

Did it make matters better or worse that he didn't seem affected? Josh was completely natural with the kids, laughing and joking as if nothing had happened. Maybe she was the only one who felt something. That should have made her feel better, but it didn't.

Their stunning victory at the gymkhana was soul satisfying, but it still left the two teams tied. That evidently hadn't occurred to the youngsters. They celebrated boisterously at dinner in town that night and were still applauding themselves over sodas after the movie.

The question of what to do about a tiebreaker was on the minds of the adults, however. Josh and Valentina met in his room to discuss the matter after they returned to the motel and sent the children to bed.

"They're so high on themselves right now," Valentina said. "I'd hate to see them suffer another humiliating defeat."

"It would destroy their budding self-respect," Josh agreed. "Probably for the first time in their lives they know what it's like to win without lying or cheating."

"What do you think Dennis and Judy will suggest for tomorrow? They're bound to want to get even."

"Something like polo, no doubt," Josh observed sardonically.

"Maybe you and I should challenge them to a race, as Gary suggested. That's the only fair thing, since they can see the children aren't evenly matched at sports."

Josh's expression changed as he looked at her. "Did you ever think we'd be on the same team?"

"Anything can happen," she said lightly. "I never expected to spend a week in the woods riding shotgun on a bunch of hyperactive kids, either."

"You're surprisingly good with them. You should have children of your own."

"You never know," she murmured vaguely, glancing away.

"You're considering it? Have you given any thought to the fact that by the time they're ready to enter high school, Warren will be in his seventies?"

"I thought we'd called a truce for this week," she pleaded.

"I'm not trying to start an argument. I'm just attempting to understand why you're marrying him."

Valentina sighed. "At least you're no longer convinced it's solely for his money. You don't still believe that, do you?"

"I'm not sure what to think anymore." Josh examined her lovely face. "I have to wonder why a woman would marry a man she's not sexually attracted to."

"You don't know that," Valentina said.

"I've watched you with Warren. You're both very affectionate toward each other—like father and daughter."

"That's not true! We aren't demonstrative in public because neither of us considers that kind of thing to be in good taste," she said stiffly.

"It didn't bother you this afternoon."

Her long lashes swept down as she remembered Josh's urgent mouth on hers—and the ardent response it provoked. Everyone else had faded into nothingness as the warmth of his body had penetrated hers.

"That was only a victory kiss," she said in a low voice.

"Was it, Valentina?" He rose and came to bend over her, grasping the arms of her chair. "Maybe it started out that way, but then something happened. I know it wasn't voluntary, but you did feel something."

She wanted to deny it, but Josh had too much experience to be deceived. "It isn't unusual for a woman to have a sexual response to an attractive man," she said dismissively. "Men don't have a corner on that. It doesn't mean a thing."

"I'm sure it's a common experience with a lot of women, but I don't think you're one of them. You're wary of any kind of physical contact, even when it's only casual."

"I don't like to be touched," she said primly.

"That wasn't the impression I got this afternoon. When was the last time you made love?" he asked unexpectedly.

Valentina stood abruptly. "I find that question in very bad taste."

"Admittedly, but it would answer something that puzzles me. Do you really find me attractive, or are you just

frustrated? You told me you and Warren aren't sleeping together.''

Josh had moved back only minimally. He was close
enough to set her nerve ends quivering. She pushed past him
and started toward the door. ''My love life is none of your
business.''

''It is if I'm part of your fantasies.'' He grinned.

''You aren't!'' She reached for the doorknob, but Josh
put his hand over hers.

''Give Warren a break,'' he said, his smile vanishing.
''Maybe I'm not the one for you, but somewhere out there
is a man who is. Warren deserves a wife who wants him in
every way.''

''That's exactly what he's going to get, in spite of what
you think.'' She brushed his hand away and opened the
door.

Valentina was already deeply troubled over the afternoon's incident, and it didn't help matters to have Josh
practically accuse her of being in love with him.

''I wouldn't touch that man with a forked stick,'' she
muttered. ''He's nothing but a glitzier version of Robert.
None of them can be trusted.''

Josh was slick, she had to give him that. He'd conned her
into thinking of him as a friend, while all the time he was
only looking for a way to talk her out of her coming marriage. That hurt more than she cared to admit.

''I'll get through this week somehow,'' she declared,
climbing into bed and yanking the covers up to her chin.
''But this is Josh's last shot at me!''

One problem was solved the next morning. Judy and
Dennis and their brood weren't in the dining room. They
turned up in the lobby a little later with their entire camp
and piles of luggage.

''Are you going somewhere?'' Josh asked.

''There isn't really enough for the children to do here,''
Dennis said. ''I made a few calls and found someplace more
suitable.''

"I'm sorry to hear that. I thought we just had a very eventful day," Josh said blandly.

"Yes, well, I'm sure it seemed that way to *your* children."

"It did. They thoroughly enjoyed yesterday's simple pleasures. Too bad your kids didn't."

"I have to check out now," Dennis said stiffly.

As he walked away Valentina said to Josh, "So much for good sportsmanship. I notice he didn't even mention the award ceremony."

"I didn't want to remind him. I figured it was better to quit while we were ahead." Josh grinned.

"I guess you're right," she agreed.

"Now that the pressure is off, I believe our group could benefit from some swimming lessons. Were you really on the swim team in college?"

"I don't lie, contrary to what you think," she said coolly.

"I never thought you did. I'm not your enemy, Valentina," he said gently. "Your problems are all of your own making."

"I don't have any problems," she answered, lifting her chin in the air and walking away.

In spite of Valentina's reservations, the week was surprisingly enjoyable. The children provided a buffer between Josh and her, although he didn't attempt to get personal again. Valentina was tense around him initially, but he was so completely natural that she relaxed, too.

It was difficult not to when they worked side by side, teaching the youngsters how to stroke instead of thrash around in the swimming pool. They also worked on their manners and grammar.

"Everybody I know understands me," Meg said pugnaciously. "Why do I need to talk like those feebs from Camp Wildwood?"

"Because they're the ones who will get the good jobs," Josh answered calmly. "Employers look for people who can express themselves clearly. Do you want to work for minimum wages all your life?"

"Okay, so that makes sense, but why do I have to open a door for some broad?" Gary asked. "What's the matter, can't she figure it out for herself?"

"*Broad* is just as unacceptable to a woman as *boy* is to a man," Valentina said crisply. "And opening a door for someone—woman or man—is a simple courtesy. Good manners are the mark of a civilized society."

The children argued out of habit, but the instruction sank in. Little by little they stopped using four-letter words and disparaging references to things they didn't like. The older ones also helped the younger ones, instead of telling them to get lost. For the first time in their lives, they started to think of somebody other than themselves.

Valentina was jubilant. "We're really getting through to them!" she told Josh.

"It certainly looks that way. I'm ashamed that I had to be coerced into coming here. I'm going to talk to Warren about staying involved. How about you?"

"Me, too." How could she refuse?

The night before they were due to leave, Valentina and Josh promised the children a gala party. He rented a jukebox and arranged with the management to clear some of the tables from the dining room to make space for dancing.

In the morning they all went into town and bought new clothes for the children. This shopping excursion was markedly different from the first one. Although the youngsters were in high spirits, they didn't strike terror in the hearts of the shop owners.

After everyone was outfitted, Josh took them all to the variety store, where they bought balloons and crepe paper. The afternoon was spent decorating the dining room. Everyone took part, and when they were finished, it looked very festive.

Anticipation ran high, and nobody complained about taking a bath. Valentina had a warm sense of accomplishment as she dressed for the evening. She and Josh had brought only jeans and T-shirts, so they also purchased new outfits. Hers was a rose-colored pair of silk pants and a pink blouse, and he bought a pair of white slacks and a navy silk shirt.

Valentina was applying lipstick when Meg knocked on the door. The youngster had on perhaps her first pair of panty-hose under a short skirt and printed blouse.

"You look great!" Valentina exclaimed.

"I look like a geek." The young girl's mouth curled.

"How can you say that? A lot of girls older than you would be happy to have your figure."

"I guess I look okay from the neck down," Meg agreed grudgingly. "It's this face I'm stuck with. Maybe I should just wear a paper bag over my head."

"You have a very pretty face. The only thing you need is a new hairdo. Come into the bathroom and I'll put some curlers in your hair."

Meg made token protests, but she watched avidly as Valentina rolled her lank hair on curlers and then dried it with a hair dryer.

The result surprised even Valentina. When she brushed Meg's hair afterward, it formed a softly curling blond halo, accentuating her brown eyes and well-shaped features.

The young girl gazed at herself, wide-eyed. "Wow! Is that really me?"

"The way you were meant to be," Valentina assured her. "You're something special. Don't ever forget that."

Gary's mouth dropped open uncharacteristically when he saw Meg. He was almost unrecognizable, too, in neat clothes, with his unruly hair combed.

"You're not half bad, kid," he said.

Instead of snapping back at him as she would have in the past, Meg gazed at him from under lowered lashes and murmured, "Thanks. You're not too shabby yourself."

"My God, they were both replaced by aliens when we weren't looking," Josh murmured in Valentina's ear.

"Let's hope they don't bring them back." She smiled.

The evening was a great success. Everybody danced, even the younger children, albeit with much giggling. Dinner was served buffet-style, which wasn't fully appreciated.

"This is just like down at the soup kitchen," Tony observed in disappointment.

"It might surprise you to know that the cocktail buffet is a staple of high society," Valentina told him.

"Why would anyone want to stand in line to get their own food if they didn't have to?" he asked.

"For the same reason they think it's fun to stand around all night with a watery drink in their hands, making boring small talk," Josh answered dryly.

"I guess we goofed on dinner," Valentina said to Josh a little later when they were dancing.

"Not necessarily. They might as well see what's ahead of them if they get rich and famous."

"Are you encouraging them to drop out?" She laughed.

"I'd say we can be proud of our efforts." He glanced approvingly over the little group.

"I think they taught us as much as we taught them," Valentina said softly.

"Did you learn some new words?" he teased. .

"You know what I mean. This week changed my mind about a lot of things."

His jaw set. "I'd like to think so."

Valentina knew they were no longer talking about the children. "Please, Josh, it's almost over. Can't we pretend to be friends for one more night?"

He stared at her moodily. "It wasn't a pretense—at least on my part. That's what bothers me."

"You'd prefer to dislike me?"

A mask descended over his face, leaving it expressionless. "I'd prefer that you didn't marry Warren."

Valentina knew they were headed for another pointless argument, so she walked away. Preventing her marriage had become an obsession with Josh. Was he really that concerned about Warren, or did he just hate to lose? Maybe it wasn't anything personal. She sighed unconsciously.

Chapter Five

Valentina was distant toward Josh for a short time, but everyone else was having such a good time that she soon forgot her grievance. By the end of the evening she and Josh were back on their old footing.

From past experience she didn't expect the rapport to last, but the children kept them too busy to think about themselves. The party lasted until late, and the next morning was hectic. Getting a dozen kids packed and ready to leave after lunch wasn't easy.

Valentina was folding a sweater to put in a suitcase when Meg came to her room. The young girl seemed to have something on her mind that she was having trouble voicing.

"Are you all packed?" Valentina asked.

"Yeah, I guess so."

"I don't know about anybody else, but I had a good time last night," Valentina remarked, to give the girl time to open up.

"Yeah, it wasn't half bad." Meg slanted a look at her. "You and Josh are okay."

Valentina was touched, realizing that was high praise. "We try hard," she said lightly.

"You're lucky. He's really hooked on you."

"As I told you, we're just friends."

"Oh, sure! That's why he can't stay away from you."

"You're imagining things. Maybe the fact that I'm en gaged to marry his best friend will convince you."

"You're kidding! The guy must be nuts to let you spen a week with a hunk like Josh."

"It was his idea." Before Meg could pursue the matter Valentina changed the subject. "I guess you'll be glad to g back to the city."

Meg's mouth twisted sardonically. "Oh, sure, the mayor waiting to meet me with a brass band."

"Your friends and family will be glad to see you."

"I live in a foster home. All my 'family' cares about whether they'll get paid for the week I was gone."

"I'm sure you mean more to them than that," Valentin protested.

"Who are you kidding? But, hey, it's okay. Pretty soo I'll be on my own, and then I won't have to report to any body."

"What do you plan to do with your life?" Valentin asked quietly.

Meg shrugged. "People like me don't plan. Things ju: happen to us—mostly bad things."

"It doesn't have to be that way. You're a very bright gi and a born leader. You can be anything you choose."

"Like a brain surgeon, I suppose?" Meg asked sarcast cally.

"If that's what you really want. Don't ever put yoursel down. You have to believe in yourself, or nobody else will."

"What difference does it make to you? We're never g ing to see each other again."

"I hope that isn't true."

"Don't try to con me. You did your good deed. Now yo can go back and tell all your rich friends what a drag thi week was."

"Do you really think I'd do a thing like that?"

"Well . . . maybe you won't rap us too bad."

"Whether you believe it or not, I enjoyed this week—an not because I was doing a so-called good deed."

Meg grinned unexpectedly. "I bet Josh had something to do with it."

"You're impossible!" Valentina laughed helplessly. "Okay, you win. I'm in love with him. Is that what you want to hear? Now go and finish packing. We have to vacate the rooms by noon."

Meg started for the door, but stopped in the entry. Whatever she wanted to say proved too difficult to express. "Thanks for the use of the curlers last night," she said finally.

"No sweat." Valentina matched the girl's offhand tone.

Josh and Valentina agreed to meet at Warren's house after they dropped the children off, knowing he'd be anxious to hear how they made out.

"I see neither of you have any battle scars, so I guess it wasn't that much of a disaster," Warren commented.

"It was a remarkable experience," Valentina said.

"That could be either good or bad. How about it, Josh? Did I send you on a mission from hell? You'll tell me the truth."

"I can only speak for myself, but I had a ball."

"The children didn't give you a bad time?" Warren persisted.

"Of course they did. They're normal, healthy kids. But if I do say so myself, I handled them expertly," Josh said smugly.

Valentina gave him a laughing glance. "With a lot of help from me. You never could have kept Meg in line."

"Surely you jest." Josh grinned. "She thought I was a hunk."

"She didn't have anything to compare you to except a thirteen-year-old boy."

"You're forgetting Dennis, the menace."

Valentina's lip curled. "I hope to, in time."

Warren watched them with an indulgent expression. "I'm glad to see you two buried the hatchet. I knew you'd feel differently once you got to know each other."

Their faces sobered. "There was one young girl I took a special interest in," Valentina said hastily. "They were all great, but I think she has real potential. Maybe your foundation can do something for her."

"I don't try to influence their decisions," Warren said.

"Surely you could mention it to them. I'd like to see her go to college. That's way in the future, but if she has an incentive, she won't do something foolish like dropping out of school or getting in with a bad crowd."

"Unfortunately, peer pressure is often a stronger motivation than the promise of future benefits," Josh remarked.

"I understand that, but you can't sit back and do nothing," Valentina protested.

"I'm not disagreeing with you. I feel as strongly about Gary as you do about Meg. He could really be somebody if he cleaned up his act. I'd hate to see him end up on the wrong side of the law."

Warren was gazing at them speculatively. "There are hundreds of Megs and Garys on the streets. How would you like to sit on the Foundation board so you can do something about them?"

"I don't have any training for that kind of work," Valentina said.

"All you need is intelligence and compassion." Warren reached over and took her hand. "You have both of those." He turned to Josh. "How about you? Are you concerned enough to do something about the problem?"

Josh looked startled. "Well, sure, if I could. But I feel the way Valentina does. I don't have any training in social work. You can put me down for a healthy donation, though."

"That's the easy way out—especially if you can afford it."

"You're not being fair! Didn't I give up a week for those kids? You think it was all fun and games?"

"I'm sure there were problems, but you worked them out and even managed to have a good time."

Josh glanced warily at Valentina, then looked away quickly. "We didn't see eye to eye on everything."

"Val and I don't, either." Warren chuckled. "I'm not asking you to go on the board to be a rubber stamp for each other or for me. I'm concerned that the present members are iving in an ivory tower. You two were actually involved with he children. You know how the money should be spent."

"I have a couple of ideas," Valentina said. "Summer camp is a start, but what's being done for them the rest of he year?"

"That's what you'll find out."

"I wouldn't hesitate under different circumstances, but I have my book to finish."

"I'm not talking about a full-time job. The board meets only once a month, except for special agendas."

"How can they make timely decisions on that kind of schedule?"

"You tell *me*. I've thought for a long time that they don't accomplish enough."

"Evidently not. Okay, I'll do it!" Her eyes started to sparkle as the idea took hold.

"Splendid. You and Josh will make a formidable team."

Valentina came back to earth abruptly. The last thing she wanted was to be in constant contact with Josh. "You can't impose on him. He has a business to run."

"Nonsense. The money rolls in whether he's there or not."

"Thanks," Josh said dryly. "It's nice to know I'm a figurehead."

"I paid you a compliment," Warren said. "A good executive doesn't have to stand over his people. He motivates them to think for themselves."

"Nice recovery." Josh grinned. "All right, you conned me again." He turned to Valentina with a derisive light in his eyes. "It looks like we'll be seeing a lot of each other."

Her mind was racing, trying to find an out. Couldn't Warren see that she didn't want to be around Josh? But how could he, since they both acted as though they'd gotten to be good buddies this past week? Warren probably wanted to keep the momentum going, she thought hopelessly.

"I knew I could count on both of you," he said with satisfaction. "Your first meeting will be on Friday at five o'clock."

"Why so late?" Josh asked.

"So it won't cut too deeply into the working day. These are all busy people."

"How long do the meetings usually last?"

"What's the matter, Josh, are you afraid this will foul up your social life?" Warren chuckled. "I'm sure your date for the evening will forgive you for being late if you explain that it's for a good cause."

Valentina was annoyed. Wasn't that just like Josh, to worry that his love life would suffer? "You can make the sacrifice if I can," she said crisply.

"You're right— I'll try to be as cheerful about it as you're being," he answered mockingly.

Valentina was so busy that week, working to make up for lost time, that she managed not to think about Josh. At least, not very often. Warren reminded her on Friday morning.

"Call me after the meeting is over and give me a report," he said.

"I'll do better than that. I'll come over and give you a blow-by blow account."

"The meeting is in the city. I can't ask you to make that long round-trip twice in one day. Unless you'll agree to stay here tonight."

"You know how I feel about that. The media is still skulking around. I found a man going through my garbage can yesterday morning. Do you think their tabloid readers are really interested in what brand of cottage cheese I eat?"

"You wouldn't think so, would you? I wish there was something I could do, but the only way we can stop them is to advance our wedding date. They'll lose interest after we're married."

"Why should we be forced into something we don't want to do? I mean, like changing our plans," she corrected herself hastily. "It is annoying, but I'll survive."

"That's the spirit." Warren patted her cheek fondly. "You'd better get started. There's a lot of traffic at this hour. Give me a call when the meeting is over."

* * *

The board met in one of the plush conference rooms of a
an Francisco office building. Although Valentina arrived
arly, Josh was already there.

She felt her nerves tighten. He looked very remote in his
talian suit and expensive silk tie—a far cry from last week's
eans and T-shirts. She'd established a shaky friendship with
hat man. This one was her declared enemy.

Josh smiled, dispelling the impression. "Well, here we
re, doing Warren's dirty work again."

"I only hope it's as productive as last week."

"We did have a good time, didn't we?" he asked softly.

"There were some bad moments," she answered guard-
dly.

"When were those, Valentina—when we kissed? Surely
ou're not dwelling on such an unimportant little inci-
lent." His smile this time was sardonic.

She refused to react. "We're here to accomplish some-
hing, so I suggest we put our differences aside for the mo-
nent and try to work together for the good of the children."

"I'm willing, but I have to warn you, we aren't likely to
core any decisive victories tonight. Boards never make
uick decisions."

"I hope you're wrong. I have a few ideas I'd like to pre-
ent. Warren gave me some information on what the Foun-
lation has been doing—mostly long-range institutional
unding. That's admirable, but I'd like to see some of the
noney diverted to more direct uses."

"What did you have in mind?"

"Creating part-time jobs, for one thing, and getting the
oungsters involved in helping each other. Remember how
heir peers looked up to Meg and Gary? We can talk until
ve're blue in the face without convincing kids of anything,
out if those two tell them drugs are slow death, they're more
pt to believe them."

"True, but they can only influence their own little group
of friends. How do we reach more than that?"

"What if we funded a group of recreation centers? Places
vhere latchkey kids could go after school. They're badly
leeded to get teenagers off the streets. We could find other

young people with leadership ability, and pay them a salary to be part-time counselors."

"I like it." Josh nodded enthusiastically. "We got to Gary temporarily last week, but I've been worried about losing him over the long haul. This is made to order."

"We'll have to start small, with only one center, but when that one's a success we won't have any trouble getting further funding. I just know it will work!"

The other members of the board began to arrive, five distinguished-looking older men. They introduced themselves in a reserved manner.

"So nice to meet you, Miss Richardson," Henry Bancroft, the chairman of the board, said. "We're happy to have you here tonight to observe our operation."

"I hope to do a lot more than that, Mr. Bancroft," she answered demurely.

He and the others were shocked to find out she and Josh intended to be active participants. When Valentina proposed her ideas, they ran into a solid wall of disapproval.

"That's very interesting, young lady, but it isn't the focus of our agenda. We've always taken a somewhat broader view."

"Perhaps that's why you haven't seen what's happening on our streets," Josh said.

Things heated up after that. The older men were alternately indignant and defensive, while Valentina and Josh remained suitably respectful, yet firm.

Clayton Willetson made a steeple of his fingers. He was a portly man in his late sixties. "Unfortunately you fail to understand the importance of long-range goals."

"Those are very estimable," Valentina answered. "But sometimes we have to reorder our priorities."

"You're getting as good at doublespeak as they are," Josh murmured to her.

"I think you'll find that Warren has complete confidence in our decisions," Henry insisted.

"I'm sure that's true, but he asked us to contribute our input. I'm afraid he'd be disappointed if we failed to accomplish anything." Her voice held a hint of steel.

"We're not trying to stonewall," Clayton said hastily. "You simply don't understand the amount of work involved in setting up these youth centers you propose. None of us has the time to contribute."

"I understand completely. But the foundation has a paid staff to handle details."

"They'd still have to report to someone."

"Valentina and I can handle that," Josh offered.

The meeting finally ended with Valentina and Josh getting a grudging pledge of financing for the first center. They managed to remain dignified until they got outside, then exultation took over.

"All right!" Josh exclaimed, giving her a high five. "We did it!"

"Was there ever any doubt?" She grinned. "When we team up we're invincible."

His hilarity dimmed. "We could be," he murmured under his breath. "That's the hell of it."

She was too excited to notice. "I can't wait to tell Meg and Gary. Let's go by and take them out to dinner."

"Good idea. We can sound them out for suggestions at the same time."

Meg and Gary were as enthused about the idea as Valentina and Josh, although Gary tried to disguise the fact.

"I don't know, man," he said initially, striving to sound cool. "Saving souls might be bad for my image. I'll have to think it over."

"Get real!" Meg said. "Your image has no place to go but up. You can count me in," she told the adults. "What does the job pay?"

After Valentina and Josh had conferred and named an amount, Gary said, "Well, hell, why didn't you say so? I'm in, too."

"Only if you clean up your language," Josh said.

"Okay, okay. For that kind of bread I guess I can talk funny."

They lingered over dinner at a little restaurant south of Market Street, then stayed on long after they were finished. It was almost ten o'clock by the time they took both teenagers home. After that, Josh drove Valentina back to her car in the building parking lot.

"The kids really went for the idea," he said with gratification. "And I don't think it was only the money."

"I agree. It was the satisfaction of having adults ask for their help. It might be the first time that ever happened."

"I'd like Warren to meet them. I'll bet he'd get a kick out of those two. Perhaps we can bring them out to his place for a swim some weekend."

"Oh, good Lord! I was supposed to call Warren after the meeting!" Valentina exclaimed. "I completely forgot about him."

"That seems to happen a lot," Josh said softly.

She stiffened. "I'd hoped this project would be neutral territory. Evidently I was wrong."

"You can't expect a leopard to turn into a house cat overnight." He smiled wryly.

Or a tiger to lose his killer instinct, she thought grimly. Josh hadn't changed. He'd just switched tactics.

"Do you want to use my car phone?" he asked innocently.

"No thanks, I'll be home soon." She got into her own car and slammed the door.

He leaned down, scanning her beautiful face. "We do make a very effective couple. Think about it."

"You call yourself Warren's best friend. Think about *that*." She turned the key and drove off.

Josh remained motionless, staring after her with an enigmatic expression.

Valentina drove out to Warren's house the next day to tell him about her plan for the teenage centers. It met with his thorough approval.

"That's what I had in mind. More of a hands-on approach than they've been taking. I knew you and Josh could shake up that stuffy board."

"He was a lot of help," she admitted. "But I can handle it myself from here on. You really should let Josh off the hook."

Warren laughed. "You have a lot to learn about that young man. Nobody makes Josh do anything he doesn't want to do."

"You didn't leave him much choice. Tell him he's done his duty," Valentina said urgently.

Warren gazed at her with a slight frown. "I thought everything was going smoothly between you two. Is there something you aren't telling me?"

"No, of course not."

Strictly speaking, that was the truth. She and Josh did get along—most of the time. The sexual tension that flared up occasionally between them was merely a physical thing, like a hay fever sufferer's reaction to pollen. It wasn't worth mentioning.

"If I thought you and Josh were putting on an act for my benefit, I'd be very upset," Warren said slowly. "I'll admit I hoped working together would make you appreciate each other's good qualities, but it's by no means obligatory."

Valentina chose her words carefully. "I admire Josh for a lot of things. He has a natural rapport with young people. I only suggested releasing him from the board because I can handle the project alone now."

"I don't think you realize the amount of work involved in setting up the kind of program you propose. Josh has experience at putting together an organization. Use his expertise. I don't want you wearing yourself out on this thing," Warren said fondly.

Before she could think of an answer, Denise and Chuck came onto the patio.

"We were in the neighborhood and thought we'd stop by," Denise said gaily.

Chuck looked embarrassed. "I hope you'll excuse us for barging in this way."

"Not at all. You're always welcome," Warren said graciously.

"You see, I told you he wouldn't mind," Denise said to her husband. She immediately turned her attention to the other two. "I hoped you'd be here, too, Val. I want to find out what you're wearing to the ball."

"What ball?" Valentina asked blankly.

"The charity ball at the Fairmont on the twelfth. I read in the society column this morning that Warren is one of the sponsors. Didn't you know?"

"I help underwrite the event every year, but I never attend," Warren explained.

"All that money and you don't even get anything out of it?" Denise asked.

"Helping people is supposed to be its own reward," he answered dryly.

"There's no law against having fun while you're doing it. I was hoping we could all sit at the same table."

Warren looked faintly surprised. "You're going?" he asked Chuck.

As usual, Denise answered for her husband. "We feel it's important to support good causes," she said demurely. "Can't you get Warren to make an exception this time?" she asked Valentina. "We could have a ball—if you'll excuse the pun." She laughed at her own joke.

"Warren doesn't like those big bashes, and I'm afraid I agree with him," Valentina said.

"I'll bet most of his associates will be there," Denise persisted. "You know scads of people."

"Maybe they have something better to do that night," Chuck said uneasily. "We'd better get going. Don't you have some shopping to do?"

Denise didn't take the hint. She kept up her efforts to persuade them, despite Valentina's attempt to change the subject and Chuck's barely concealed distress.

Finally Warren took pity on his aide. "We'll consider it. Now, if you'll excuse me, I think I'll go for a swim."

After they left, Valentina said, "She doesn't let up, does she?"

"No, she's a very determined young woman, even if her priorities are skewed."

"Well, to be charitable about it, a lot of women enjoy getting all dressed up and going out on the town."

Warren raised an eyebrow. "Is that a hint?"

"No, I'm the kind who comes right out and says what's on her mind." Valentina smiled. "I was referring to Denise."

"I can understand wanting to go dancing, but five hundred dollars is a little steep for them. And that doesn't include incidentals like drinks, parking and tips."

"You mean, the ball costs five hundred dollars a couple?"

"Exactly."

"Good lord. Chuck can't afford that kind of money!"

"Not very often, anyway."

"He should practice saying no to her," Valentina declared.

"Well, maybe this is a special occasion. He did mention they have an anniversary coming up."

"That must be it."

"If you want to go, I'll take you," Warren said tepidly.

"That's really true love." She laughed. "But don't worry. I have no interest in taking you up on your offer."

Warren was right about the amount of work involved in starting a project like Valentina's, even with the help of the Foundation staff. She was faced with endless decisions that were very time-consuming. Often after a full day's work she had to rush back to the city because some crisis or other had arisen.

That's when she began to appreciate Josh's expertise. He went to the heart of a problem and pointed out how it could be solved. It took many meetings between them, but she was learning a great deal.

One late afternoon while she was hastily cleaning off her desk, Warren wandered into her office. "What's the big hurry?" he asked.

"I have a meeting with Josh and the contractors at the building site. They say the architect's blueprint calls for removing a wall that contains a support post. The plans have to be altered."

"I thought we were going to dinner and a movie tonight."

"I'm sorry, darling, but all the work will be stalled until this has been resolved."

"Can't Josh go without you?"

"The contractor wants both our signatures on the work order."

"Well, I suppose it can't be helped." Warren sighed. "But I didn't see you last night, either."

"I know. You were right when you said this was a big job."

"I think I've created a monster."

"You'll change your mind when you see how happy you've made a lot of youngsters." She kissed his cheek. "Bye, darling. See you in the morning."

Warren walked to his own office and stood by the window with his hands in his pockets, watching her drive away. His secretary paused in the doorway for a moment, then coughed to get his attention.

When he turned around she asked, "Did you want to dictate a letter to Consolidated about those memory chips?"

"It can wait until tomorrow. Why don't you go on home? It's almost quitting time."

"I've never been a clock-watcher," Florence answered.

"I'm aware of that." Warren's face softened. "I don't know what I would have done without you all those months when Marian was ill. You were always here for both of us."

"She was a wonderful woman."

"Yes." Warren sighed heavily. "I feel like a drink," he said abruptly. "Have one with me, if you're not in a hurry to leave."

She looked startled. "No, I . . . I don't have anywhere to go."

"Splendid. What can I fix you?" He opened the top half of a large globe that concealed a bar.

After Warren had mixed the drinks, Florence perched gingerly on the edge of a chair, holding her glass. "I compiled the data on the digitized imagery," she said. "I can get it for you if you want to look it over."

"Not now." He gazed at her consideringly. "We've worked together for over ten years, and it just occurred to me that I really know very little about your private life. If you don't mind my asking, have you ever been married?"

"No." She stared down at her drink. "I was engaged once, but then my mother got sick and I had to take care of her."

"Your young man objected to postponing the wedding?" he asked delicately.

"It was a long illness. She didn't pass on until a few years later. By that time ... well, he wasn't around anymore."

"I see." Warren hid his pity. "What do you like to do in your spare time?"

"I paint a little bit, although I'm not very good," she said shyly.

"I can hardly believe that. You're good at everything."

"Not at the things that count." Her face was wistful. "I can't talk to people."

"You're talking to me." He smiled.

"You're probably bored, but you're too polite to show it."

"I can't believe a competent, clever woman like you could have such an inferiority complex. You need to be more self-centered. Talk about the things that interest *you*."

"They wouldn't interest anybody else."

"You don't know that ahead of time. Try me."

"Well ... I've always been fascinated by space travel. I read about a man right here in the Silicon Valley who's building a private spaceship in his backyard. Do you think that's possible?"

"It depends on how much he knows about aerodynamics. Leonardo da Vinci envisioned the airplane. He even drew a prototype."

"Do you think we'll see colonization of outer space in our lifetime?" Florence forgot her self-consciousness.

That opened up other subjects and they talked for an hour. Finally Warren glanced at his watch. "Do you know what time it is?"

She rose immediately, her animation draining away. "I'm keeping you from something."

"Only a solitary dinner, and I hate to eat alone. I was about to suggest we go out to dinner and perhaps take in a movie afterward."

Her face turned pink with pleasure, but she said, "Do you think that would be all right?"

"Why not? You mean, because of Valentina?" Warren smiled wryly. "She's too busy these days to have time for me."

Florence's mouth firmed. "Some women don't appreciate what they have."

"You're good for my ego." He chuckled. "Just for that, I'm going to buy you the fanciest dinner in town."

Chapter Six

Valentina was determined to have the teenage center in operation by the end of summer, even though everyone said it couldn't be done. Josh helped her prove they were wrong.

It took up a great deal of time. Since each was busy during the day, a lot of the details had to be attended to after hours. Several times a week they met for working meetings over dinner.

These were valid business sessions, not dates, so Valentina had no qualms about spending so many evenings with Josh. Especially since they were careful not to get personal. Occasionally she detected a male look in his eyes as he gazed at her. Or a moment of tension would occur when their bodies touched while they were inspecting blueprints side by side. But for the most part, both tried hard to ignore the other's sexuality.

Valentina began to look forward eagerly to those evenings with Josh. She assured herself it was because the project was so worthwhile. To prove the point, she made detailed reports to Warren about everything they talked about and what progress was being made.

He didn't share her enthusiasm—at least not to the same extent. "I realize it's a good cause, but you're becoming a little obsessed. It isn't necessary for you to personally over-see every nail that's driven.''

"A lot more than remodeling is involved. When that's finished we'll need to shop for comfortable furniture and games and books. I want the place to feel like their own living room would, if they lived in a normal home.''

"Do you have to read every book before approving it?'' Warren asked caustically.

Valentina looked at him uncertainly. "I thought we were in agreement on this project. You were the one who told me to get involved.''

"I didn't realize it was going to take over your life—*our* lives. I never see you anymore.''

"I'm here every day.''

"But not at night.''

"I'll admit this has been a hectic week, but it's only for a little while longer. Everything is finally whipping into shape.''

"That will be a comforting thought when I'm having dinner alone in front of the television set,'' he said dryly.

"Do you want me to find someone to take over?'' she asked soberly.

His frown vanished as he looked at her drooping mouth. "No, honey, I'm really proud of what you've accomplished. Don't mind me. I'm just feeling cranky.''

"You have every right to.'' She put her arms around his neck. "I've been neglecting you shamelessly, but that's going to change right now. You and I are going to have a romantic candlelight dinner tonight, just the two of us.''

"How about your meeting?''

"Josh can handle it. He's awesome at dealing with people. If reason doesn't work, he charms them into doing what he wants.''

Warren looked at her speculatively. "I'm beginning to wonder if I haven't made a mistake in urging you two on each other. At first I was delighted that you were hitting it off so well, but women do find Josh irresistible.''

And vice versa, Valentina added silently. That was one of his liabilities, as far as she was concerned. Josh never mentioned his personal life, but it was obviously active. Women called him constantly on his car phone.

Valentina's gaze didn't waver. "I made my choice a long time ago, and I'm happy with it."

After her conversation with Warren, Valentina cut back drastically on her evening meetings. She would have cancelled them entirely, but he assured her he didn't mind as long as they weren't excessive.

"I can amuse myself one or two nights a week."

"Yes, but I know you don't like to eat alone."

"I don't always. Florence has taken pity on me a couple of times."

Valentina's eyebrows shot up. "Your secretary?"

"I don't blame you for being surprised. We don't think of her as being a person. She's as unobtrusive as the fax machine or the computer."

"She's certainly competent."

"Poor Florence, that's damning with faint praise, all right," Warren said wryly. "She's really a very interesting woman when you get to know her."

"I'll take your word for it. We aren't exactly soul mates."

"Probably because you represent everything she'd like to be."

"I doubt it very seriously. Where did you get that idea?"

"We've had some long conversations. She has an excellent mind and a lively imagination, but I gather she'd trade them gladly for a face and figure like yours."

"There's nothing wrong with her figure, and she could be quite attractive with some makeup and a decent hairdo," Valentina said thoughtfully.

"Maybe you could suggest it to her."

"No way! She barely tolerates me now."

"It might ease the strain between you."

"Or make it worse."

"You never know. She might surprise you by being receptive. I think Florence desperately wants to be more attractive."

"Why don't you do your own dirty work?" Valentina complained. "You're always sending me out to help the disadvantaged."

"Because you're so good at it." He gave her a melting smile.

"Oh, all right." She returned his smile ruefully. "You can always talk me into anything."

"I hope I didn't talk you into marrying me."

Valentina blotted out the image of Josh that surfaced momentarily. "That was the best decision I ever made," she said with affection.

Valentina expected Warren's secretary to reject her overtures, but a promise was a promise. After putting it off for a few days, she forced herself to stop by Florence's office.

Pausing tentatively in the doorway, she said, "I'd like to talk to you if you're not busy."

The woman glanced up warily. "I have some reports to get out."

Valentina resisted an urge to accept the reprieve. "This won't take long."

Florence's mouth thinned as Valentina walked into the room. "I suppose it's about Mr. Powell."

"Why would you think that?"

"Don't play games with me. If you have something to say, why don't you come right out and say it?"

"You're not making it easy," Valentina murmured wryly.

"Why should I? Everything always comes easy to women who look like you," Florence said bitterly.

Valentina saw her opening and took it. "I didn't think you cared about your appearance."

"What good would it do?" The older woman's fire died and her shoulders slumped.

"That's a cop-out. If you're not happy with your image, change it. You could be a lot more attractive if you cut your hair, for starters." Valentina gazed at her appraisingly. "A short feathery style would be very becoming. You should use mascara and eye shadow, too—green would be nice with your hazel eyes."

"I don't consider eye makeup appropriate for the office," Florence said primly.

"That's nonsense. You also need a brighter shade of lipstick and some clothes that aren't so earnest. It's hard to tell, but I'll bet you have a nice figure under that nondescript outfit. I don't mean to be insulting, but that suit you're wearing would lower anybody's self-esteem."

"I paid a lot of money for this suit!"

"I'm sure that's true, but you could find one equally nice that's not quite so severe. Why don't you check out some of the little shops in the village? Michele's has beautiful separates—tailored jackets with snappy pleated skirts to mix or match. But for heaven's sake, wear them short enough to show off your legs. They're really quite good."

"Why are you telling me all this?" Florence asked slowly.

"Because I think it would give you a whole new outlook—a rosier one. Happy people are easier to get along with." Valentina smiled. "Since we're both part of Warren's life, it would be nice if we could be friends."

"I thought you were angry that Mr. Powell took me out to dinner."

"Certainly not. I'm grateful to you for keeping him company."

Florence's mouth twisted in self-mockery. "I guess that *was* foolish of me. Why would a man like Mr. Powell look twice at me when he's engaged to someone like you?"

"You really have to stop putting yourself down. And another thing. Don't you think it's time you started calling him Warren? Everybody else does."

"He told me to, but I feel funny about it," Florence said shyly.

"Work on it." Valentina walked to the door.

It had turned out to be a very satisfactory conversation. Florence had been more receptive than she'd expected. Valentina only hoped the older woman would take the advice and break out of her shell. Florence could have a full life instead of pouring all of her energy into her job. Maybe she'd even find romance.

* * *

A few days later Warren told Valentina he had to go to Washington, D.C. for a week.

"I'd ask you to come with me, but I wouldn't be able to spend much time with you. I'll be in contract meetings with the government every day," he explained.

"Now who's deserting whom?" she teased.

"Not by choice, I assure you. I'd love to have you along, but you'd be on your own most of the time, and it's hot and humid in Washington at this time of year," he warned.

"That's not much of a recommendation. I'll stay home and work on my book."

"You'll also have time to devote to the Foundation."

"I *have* been dumping most of it on Josh lately," she admitted.

"You'll be too busy to miss us," Warren assured her.

"Us?"

"Florence is going with me. I could hire a temp in Washington, but there will be a lot of changes in the contracts, and I want to be sure the figures I rework are accurate. She knows the percentages better than I do."

"Too bad she isn't as sharp about herself. I had a talk with her, as you suggested. She seemed receptive, but so far I haven't noticed any change."

"Well, at least you tried." Warren dismissed the matter.

Since Warren was out of town there was no reason for Valentina to drive to his house every day. She could work at home just as well. Her apartment seemed very quiet, though, after all the activity there.

And the nights were lonely. She felt diffident about calling Josh and resuming their evening meetings. He seemed to be managing fine without her.

A few days after Warren left, Josh phoned. "I just called Warren's house and discovered he's out of town and you aren't coming around anymore. What gives?"

"He's away on business, and I'm working at home this week, that's all."

"I see. Well, that clears up the mystery."

Before he could end the conversation, she said. "I presume everything is going smoothly on the project. I haven't heard from you in a long time."

"That should make you happy." His voice was dry.

She chose to ignore it. "I'm sorry about leaving you to shoulder the burden, but it was unavoidable."

"How about making up for it this week?"

"Well, sure, I'd be happy to. What can I do?"

"Have dinner with me tonight." When she hesitated, Josh said quickly, "I'd like you to look at some job applications with me. There are a couple of borderline cases and I'd appreciate your input."

Valentina felt her heart lift. "Anytime you say."

"Good. I'll pick you up at seven-thirty."

As she applied mascara to her long lashes that night, Valentina was as excited as a schoolgirl preparing for her first date. Which was a ridiculous analogy, she told herself. This wasn't a date, and she was merely pleased at getting her project back.

The first sight of Josh took her breath away momentarily. She'd almost forgotten how overwhelmingly male he was. His beige linen suit jacket emphasized the width of his shoulders, and he seemed even taller than usual in her small apartment.

"You're very dressed up for a dinner meeting," she managed finally.

"No more than you are." His topaz eyes traveled over her admiringly.

"This old thing?" she said dismissively. The pale blue silk dress was a simple sheath, but it clung to her curves in all the right places. "Would you like a drink?"

"We can have one at the restaurant. I made a reservation at Trader Tommy's, if that's all right with you."

"It's perfect. I love those fancy drinks they make with a paper parasol on top. Their Singing Missionary tastes just like chilled fruit juice."

"With a kick afterward that tells you what the missionaries are singing about." Josh chuckled.

* * *

The restaurant had a tropical decor. Fishing nets were draped on the walls, and giant clam shells held imitation pearls. In the busy bar off the main entry, people sat on rattan stools and sipped drinks served by bartenders in tropical shirts.

When they were seated in the dining room, Valentina glanced around happily. "This is what I imagine Tahiti is like."

"It's a little more plush here."

"You've been to Tahiti?"

Josh nodded. "A couple of years ago."

"Was it very romantic?"

"Anyplace is romantic if you're with the right person," he said softly.

Valentina gazed down at the coconut half that held her drink. "Were you?"

"Was I what?"

"With the right person."

"Obviously not."

"Why obviously?"

"Because I wouldn't be here with you this evening—which would be a pity."

"Tonight doesn't count. This is a business meeting."

"I tend to forget business when I'm with a beautiful woman."

"Even one who's engaged to your best friend?"

The glow in Josh's eyes cooled perceptibly. "She isn't married yet."

"We seem to be right back where we started. Perhaps this dinner was a mistake."

He covered her hand with his. "I'm sorry if I stepped over the line again, but you know how I hate to lose."

"Yes." She stifled a sigh. In spite of the flowery compliments and male admiration, that was the basis of their entire relationship.

"What would you like to eat?" He handed her one of the menus the waiter had left. "The lamb with peanut sauce is always good."

Valentina was on guard at first, but Josh could charm a traffic cop when it suited him. Playing on her interest in Tahiti, he talked about another trip he'd taken to the South Seas, and the exotic places he'd visited, like Fiji and Pago Pago. Her reserve was soon forgotten as she peppered him with questions.

"Were you on a cruise?" she asked.

"No, I don't care for cruises. They don't allow enough time ashore. I prefer to stay long enough to get to know the natives and see how they live."

"Yours is the ideal way. I wonder why more people don't do it?"

"Either they don't want to put forth the effort or they're afraid to try it, which is foolish. You just need to use a little common sense." Josh started to laugh. "I heard about a couple who made their first trip to Europe, intending to travel through several countries by train. Friends told them horror stories about luggage being stolen on the platform, so the woman got on the train with as much as she could carry, leaving her husband to struggle with the rest of their bags. What they should have been told—besides not to overpack—was that Swiss trains leave exactly on time."

"Don't tell me she left without him!"

"Unavoidably." Josh chuckled. "Not only that, he was carrying all their money and passports, and she didn't speak anything but English."

"What happened?"

"It took him four hours to locate her, but everything worked out all right. Most things do."

"That's the way I've always felt. You shouldn't be afraid to take chances. Who knows? Your entire life could change for the better."

"Or not." His laughter died abruptly as he gazed at her finely chiseled profile.

"I wish you'd pick one side and stick to it. I was agreeing with you." She glanced up from her plate with a smile.

"I wish I could convince you that you're making a mistake with *your* life," he said grimly.

Her smile faded. "You can't say it's for lack of trying."

Josh's face cleared. "Okay, you win some, you lose some," he said lightly.

Valentina wasn't fooled into thinking he'd given up, but she didn't want to argue. "We're supposed to be discussing the center. How does it look now that the furniture is in? They did deliver it, didn't they?"

"Just yesterday. I haven't seen it yet myself."

"If all the furniture and equipment are there, we can open soon." Her eyes sparkled with pleasure. "How about that? We're way ahead of schedule."

"Not exactly. We have to wait for a final inspection."

"How long can that take?" she asked dismissively. "A couple of days?"

"Try a few weeks."

"You have to be joking!" Valentina exclaimed.

"That's if we're lucky. It's more apt to be a month or more."

"What could possibly take so long? The city sends a man out. If there's anything wrong, we bring it up to code. End of discussion."

"You have a lot to learn about bureaucracy. One government agency has to inform another, and all of them have to issue ten-page memos before they can even consider scheduling an inspection."

"That's ridiculous!" she fumed.

"*You* know it, and *I* know it, but nobody told the government."

"Isn't there anything you can do to speed up the process? You have influence."

"Ask me for something easy—like tickets to the Super Bowl on the fifty-yard line," Josh said wryly.

"You mean, there's nothing we can do?"

"Practice patience is all I can suggest."

"I suppose I'll have to." Valentina sighed. "How does the clubhouse look now that the furniture is in? I haven't been there in ages."

"Would you like to stop by after dinner?"

"I'd love to," she said eagerly.

* * *

The buildings around the center were dark and faintly intimidating. This wasn't the best neighborhood, but they'd had no choice. It was where inner-city children lived and played. When the clubhouse opened, it would get some of them off the streets, Valentina hoped.

She watched as Josh unlocked double locks on the front door. "Is that enough protection?" she asked. "We have a lot of equipment in there."

"A security guard makes regular rounds to check on the place," he answered.

The large area was as inviting as a recreation room in a private home. Comfortable couches and chairs were arranged in groups at one end, and a standing card table held boxes of games like Trivial Pursuit and Jeopardy. Across the room was a big-screen television set with a VCR and a stack of cassettes on top. One wall was completely covered with built-in bookcases stacked with books, and a small alcove held a computer and printer. In the center of the room was a Ping-Pong table.

"This is fantastic!" Valentina exclaimed. "It's exactly the way I hoped it would be."

"I can't think of anything we overlooked," Josh said with satisfaction. "There's something for everybody."

"The place will be packed every day," she predicted happily. "The only thing I'm having second thoughts about is the Ping-Pong table. Will it disrupt the groups at either end when the ball goes flying into their midst?"

"That's a good question. Let's try it out and see."

"Why not?" Valentina picked up a paddle. "Are you any good?"

He grinned. "You never let me show you."

"Keep your mind on the game or I'll beat your socks off."

"Don't bet on it," Josh answered as he took off his jacket and rolled up his shirtsleeves.

At first he lobbed easy shots across the net that a beginner couldn't miss. But when she made slashing returns, aiming for the edge of the table, his eyes narrowed and he began to play in earnest.

Josh was a superb athlete, even at Ping-Pong. Valentina was run ragged as he controlled the rally, expertly placing the ball on alternate sides of the table. She gave him a good game, but he won decisively.

"Does that answer your question?" he asked smugly.

"It wasn't a fair contest," she complained. "I'm wearing high heels."

"No excuses. Just admit you were outclassed."

"Never! I'd like to see *you* play in these shoes."

"Since that's impractical, why don't you take them off and I'll give you a rematch? I warn you, though, I'll expect an apology when you lose again."

"In your dreams!" she hooted.

Valentina's excuse was valid. They were more evenly matched in the second game. The lead seesawed back and forth as both gave it their total effort. She finally scored the winning point with a delicate shot that dropped just over the net when Josh was expecting a smash.

"Did I hear something about an apology?" she crowed.

"I think I've just been had. You were holding back the first time."

"Is it so hard to admit you were beaten by a woman?"

Josh smiled as he laid down his paddle and went around to her side of the table. "I always told you a man is no match for a smart woman."

"This wasn't a battle of the sexes," she protested. "It was a test of skill. And just to prove I didn't win by a fluke, I'll give you another chance."

"That won't be necessary." He brushed the damp hair off her forehead. "I bow to your superiority."

"That's very gallant of you, but it hasn't been proven yet. We're tied, one game apiece. We have to play the tiebreaker to determine who's the champion."

"I think we should quit while we can both claim a victory."

"I can't believe you're afraid of losing."

His laughter died as he gazed at her flushed face. "Believe it," he said soberly.

The atmosphere between them became charged, as it had at the beginning of the evening. Valentina tried to prevent the tension from escalating. "Sometimes you just have to accept things," she said lightly, turning away.

Josh hooked a hand around the nape of her neck, pulling her back to face him. "Not when you know they're wrong."

"Maybe you're right about quitting while we're tied," she said carefully. "We have a better chance of remaining friends that way."

"Don't pretend you don't know what I'm talking about. What do I have to do to shake some sense into you?"

Valentina gave up the pretense. "We were getting along so well," she said in a low voice. "Do you *like* arguing with me?"

"If that's what it takes," he answered grimly.

"You're obviously not going to get anywhere. We've been over the same ground a million times."

"And you refuse to listen. Words don't seem to penetrate that stubborn, closed mind of yours." Josh's eyes glittered and his jaw set as he jerked her toward him. "Maybe I should demonstrate one reason why you shouldn't marry Warren."

They were so close that she could feel the heat emanating from his taut body. He was blatantly masculine with his shirt unfastened and curly dark hair showing in the opening. Something stirred in her midsection, but she fought mightily to ignore it.

"Whatever you have in mind, I'm not interested," she said coldly.

"Are you sure, Valentina?" he asked softly, sliding his arms around her. "There's an awesome physical attraction between us. If you're honest with yourself, you'll admit it."

She braced her palms against his chest to keep distance between their bodies. "You have an ego bigger than Pittsburgh! Let go of me this instant!"

He drew her closer instead. "You're trembling. Are you afraid I might kiss you? Why does that throw you into such a panic?"

"It should be obvious, even to you!"

"A lot of things are clear to me." He gazed hypnotically into her wide blue eyes. "You're a warm, passionate woman. How long has it been since you were kissed properly? I'm not talking about a little peck on the cheek."

"You have no right to ask that," she answered breathlessly.

"Let's just say I take a personal interest in you." His fingers combed through her long, tawny hair as one arm tightened around her waist. "You can't keep perfectly normal feelings bottled up forever."

"I suppose you'd consider making love to me an act of charity." She managed to sound scornful, but her heart was hammering so loudly she was afraid he might hear it.

"I'd consider it a rare privilege." Josh's lips brushed over hers in a feathery caress that left her wanting more.

Much more. A torrent of emotions raced through Valentina's heated body. Feelings she'd thought were safely submerged now surfaced demandingly. For one insane moment she wanted to fling her arms around Josh's neck and let him satisfy the craving deep within her.

When his embrace tightened and his mouth closed over hers she stiffened, but only initially. The seduction of his lips, his hard male body, the tactile feeling of lithe muscles under smooth skin, was too much to resist. With a sigh of pleasure she wound her arms around his neck and allowed her body to conform to his.

The pressure of his mouth increased as he parted her lips and probed the moist opening, uttering a low growl of satisfaction. His hands wandered restlessly over her back, sending little thrills up Valentina's spine. After a torrid moment Josh lifted her into his arms without releasing her mouth, and carried her over to the couch.

A tiny voice sounded a warning in her ear when he lay down beside her, but it wasn't nearly as clamorous as the excitement Josh was generating. How could she deny what she wanted so badly? His kiss was smolderingly sensuous, a tantalizing taste of how masterfully he would make love.

"Beautiful Valentina," he muttered. "You're like a fever in my blood. I want to kiss every inch of your beautiful body and make you mine. You want me, too, don't you, angel?"

"Yes," she whispered, unable to deny what was so throbbingly evident.

"I knew it!" he said exultantly. "I couldn't be wrong about you."

She pulled his head down and murmured, "Kiss me."

"Yes, darling, anything you want."

Their kisses grew in intensity until both were taut with desire. Josh's hands caressed her, trailing paths of fire that threatened to flare out of control. Valentina arched her body into his hard frame in an effort to get even closer, although there was only one way.

"Sweet Valentina, I don't know how much longer I can hold back," he groaned.

Before she could answer, the doorknob rattled and a voice called loudly, "Who's in there? Open up!"

Josh and Valentina gazed at each other in mute protest. When the security guard began to pound on the door, Josh smoothed her tousled hair gently before getting up and going to the door.

Valentina's first reaction had been a profound sense of regret at the interruption. That was followed by horror at her own behavior. How could she have surrendered with hardly a struggle? No wonder Josh doubted her integrity. She could barely look at him when he returned from reassuring the guard that their presence was legitimate.

"I'm sorry," he said quietly.

She nodded silently, then turned away. "Please take me home."

"First we have to talk. I never meant for this to happen." Deep lines were carved in his rugged face. "I don't know how ... I mean, I would never ..."

"Let's just go," she said miserably.

After a moment's hesitation he sighed deeply. "Yes, I guess we'd better."

They didn't speak in the car, and when they reached her apartment, she got out hurriedly before Josh could walk her to the door.

His eyes were bleak as he watched her disappear into the building. "Goodbye, Valentina," he muttered. "It's been hell knowing you."

* * *

The telephone startled Valentina when it rang early the next morning, but it didn't awaken her. She hadn't slept all night.

Warren's voice was hearty. After telling her how much he missed her, he said, "I'm sorry to call so early, but I wanted to be sure to catch you in. I forgot all about an industry awards dinner I was supposed to attend tonight in Palo Alto. You'll have to go in my place. Get Josh to take you."

"I don't want to go without you," she said swiftly.

"That's sweet, honey, but they're giving me a silly plaque or something. You have to be there to accept it for me."

"Let Josh do it."

"You're the one they want to see more than either of us." Warren chuckled. "Besides, Josh is getting his own award."

"Then he can pick up yours at the same time."

"I know these things are boring, but I'd really appreciate it if you'd do this for me, sweetheart."

She tried desperately to get out of it. "I won't know anybody there," she pleaded. "Why don't you ask Chuck to fill in for you? Denise would adore it."

"They'll be there, but I'd prefer to have you accept the award. I like to show you off," he said fondly. "Of course if you're that set against it, I certainly won't force you to go." His voice held disappointment, however.

Valentina was caught in a dilemma. Warren gave so much and asked so little for himself. How could she turn him down without a more valid reason than she'd given?

"I didn't realize it was that important to you. Naturally I'll go," she said, trying not to let her misery show.

"I'd really appreciate it, sweetheart. Give Josh a call."

"I can't ask him to come all the way into the city to pick me up and then take me back again. I can go by myself."

"I don't want you driving alone late at night. Why don't you stay at my house tonight? Then he'd only have to make one trip in. I know Josh wouldn't mind."

"That's an idea," she said vaguely. "Don't worry, I'll work it out."

Warren's suggestion about staying at his house overnight was a good one, but Valentina had no intention of even speaking to Josh. Either that night or any other time in the future, if she could avoid it.

Chapter Seven

Valentina approached the awards dinner that night with all the reluctance of a French aristocrat going to the guillotine. Judging by the noise coming from the dining room, the event had attracted a large crowd, but it was too much to expect that she and Josh wouldn't meet. How could she possibly face him?

What happened the night before wasn't solely her fault, she reminded herself, but it wasn't much consolation. Drawing a deep breath, she went inside.

The room held a sea of unfamiliar faces, adding to her insecurity. As she hovered uncertainly in the doorway, Chuck and Denise came over to her. For once, Valentina was actually happy to see the other woman.

Denise scrutinized her from head to toe, as usual. "That's a knockout dress," she said.

Valentina hadn't wanted to wear anything too flamboyant, but on the other hand, she wanted to do Warren proud. She'd finally settled on a high-necked, long-sleeved black sheath that fit closely to below her hips. A wide black organza ruffle flared out at the short hem, layered over a white ruffle that peeked out from underneath.

"I'll show you where our table is," Chuck said.

"It's right up in front," Denise said happily. "Some of the real movers and shakers are sitting with us, too."

"I asked Josh to join us, but he said he'd already made other arrangements," Chuck said.

Valentina followed them without comment, thanking heaven for small blessings. Her relief was short-lived. Josh's table was next to theirs.

Her pulse sped up at the first glimpse of him. He was laughing with the woman next to him, completely relaxed and enjoying himself. Last night had been only an unfortunate incident to him, Valentina thought bitterly. She looked away and pinned a smile on her face as Chuck introduced her to the other people at the table.

Josh's face sobered when he caught sight of her. He made an excuse to his partner and rose, obviously intending to come over and speak to her, but Valentina pushed her chair back hurriedly and fled to the ladies' room. When she returned, everyone was seated and dinner was being served.

It was an uncomfortable meal. Valentina was conscious of Josh's steady gaze, although she never looked in his direction. While dessert was being served, an orchestra started to play. Why didn't they give out the awards and be done with it? she thought despairingly. Her misery deepened when Josh appeared beside her. It was too much to hope that she could avoid him all evening.

"I didn't expect you to be here," he said.

"It isn't by choice," she answered curtly. "Warren asked me to come."

"That didn't occur to me." Josh stared at her somberly. "Would you care to dance?"

"You must be joking!"

"We have to talk, Valentina, and I don't imagine you want to do it here," he said in a low voice.

She glanced over to see Denise watching them avidly. "Maybe later."

"It won't get any easier." He took her hand and drew her to her feet.

Valentina held herself tensely as Josh took her in his arms on the dance floor, although he left plenty of space be-

tween them. "Why don't they start the program?" she asked
tautly. "They usually do it right after dinner."

"They're waiting for the president of the association to
get here. His plane was late."

"This thing could last for hours!"

He dismissed that and got right to the point. "I want to
apologize for my behavior last night. It was never my intention to make love to you."

That didn't make her feel a lot better. "We must have a
different definition of the act," she said coldly.

His mouth twisted wryly. "You're irresistibly alluring."

"Are you trying to say I seduced you? It was the other
way around!"

He shook his head. "What happened between us was
completely spontaneous. I feel as guilty over it as you do.
Warren is my friend. I would never betray his trust."

"Exactly what *were* you trying to do?" Valentina demanded.

"In my lamebrained way I was attempting to demonstrate that if other men could arouse you, then you weren't
ready to marry Warren."

"That's contemptible!"

"It seemed like a good idea at the time." He sighed. "I
didn't reckon with the awesome chemistry between us."

"Physical attraction is simply a reflex action. It can happen between people who don't even like each other—like us.
It doesn't mean a thing," she insisted.

"We might be adversaries, but I don't think you can say
we don't like each other. We've shared a lot of good times."

"And a lot of bad ones. How can you be friends with
somebody you don't approve of?"

"Which one of us are you talking about?" He smiled.

"Don't play games with me! You've been against my
marriage from the beginning. Is that a mark of friendship?"

"I believed I was doing what was best for both of you,"
he said slowly. "In the beginning I thought you were after
Warren's money. I realized I was wrong after I got to know
you, but I still thought you were marrying him for the wrong
reasons. I haven't changed my mind about that. I have a

feeling it's tied in with something that happened to you in the past."

"That's nonsense! Warren is a wonderful man. You should be the first person to recognize it."

"I do. That's why I want to keep him from being hurt." Josh scanned Valentina's delicate face, lingering on her soft mouth. "But perhaps I've been guilty of tunnel vision. Being married to you might be worth some ultimate pain. You're enchanting enough to make any man willing to chance it." He touched the corner of her mouth in a fleeting caress.

She jerked her head away. "Is this another of your tricks? Pretending to switch sides?"

"No more tricks, Valentina. I wish things could have been different for us. I wish I'd met you before Warren did, but it wasn't meant to be, so I'll just have to accept the fact."

She didn't trust him for an instant. "That shouldn't be difficult. You don't want me or any other woman on a long-term basis."

"I won't argue, because I've never succeeded in convincing you of anything. I just wanted to tell you I'm sorry about last night, and for what it's worth, I withdraw all my objections."

"You're throwing in the towel, just like that?"

He smiled faintly. "You're the undisputed winner. I'm getting out of your life. From now on, I won't keep turning up to annoy you."

It was what she'd professed to want, so why did the idea cause a sharp pain in her breast? "I don't want to break up your friendship with Warren," she said quickly. "You can still come over to swim on the weekend."

Josh shook his head. "We'd both feel awkward with each other."

"He'll suspect something is wrong if you never come around," she persisted. "He'll think we had a falling-out."

"Leave it to me. I'll make sure he doesn't blame you."

"That wasn't my sole concern," she murmured.

"What is?" He looked at her sharply. "I'm giving you what you want. Are you having second thoughts about your marriage?"

"No, certainly not. I just—" She gave a shaky laugh. "I guess I've simply gotten used to having you around."

"Like a bad rash?" he asked dryly.

"You know that isn't what I meant. I suppose in spite of everything, we *have* gotten to be friends."

"And the only way we'll stay that way is if we don't see each other anymore." His lips brushed her temple. "Have a good life, Valentina."

The rest of the evening was torture for Valentina. She had to make small talk while her mind was in turmoil. Eventually Denise noticed.

"Is anything wrong?" she asked. "It's such a great party, but you don't seem to be enjoying yourself."

Valentina forced a smile. "I'm worried about my acceptance speech. I hate getting up in front of a lot of people."

"Don't worry about it. The women won't be paying attention to anything but your dress."

"And the men will be looking at your figure." Chuck smiled. "You're bound to be a hit."

Eventually the program began. Valentina accepted the plaque on Warren's behalf in a few gracious words, trying to ignore Josh's steady gaze. Courtesy demanded that she stay through the rest of the awards, but as soon as they were over she excused herself.

"You're not leaving already?" Denise objected. "The orchestra will be back for more dancing."

"It's a school night," Valentina joked. "I have to go home."

"It's time we were leaving, too," Chuck said.

Denise looked at her watch. "It isn't even midnight yet. You two are a couple of party poopers."

"Val and I have to go to work in the morning," he said.

"Big deal! Another hour won't make that much difference. I bought a new dress for this occasion."

"You can wear it when we go to the Ritz Carlton next week," he told her placatingly.

Valentina didn't wait to see who would win the argument. It was a foregone conclusion. Before Denise could embroil her in it, she left.

* * *

Valentina got undressed in Warren's guest room and climbed wearily into bed. It had been a grueling evening, coming on top of last night's trauma. But at least it was all over now.

That had such a final sound. What would it be like without Josh to argue with constantly? He'd made her life a living hell at times, but he'd also given it spice. There would be no more joking around the pool on weekends, no more meetings about the center. One or the other of them would have to leave the board.

Valentina stared somberly into the darkness, knowing she was evading the truth. Those weren't the things she'd miss. The terrible truth was, she'd fallen in love with Josh, and the thought of never being with him again was tearing her apart.

Under the circumstances, she couldn't possibly marry Warren. Was that Josh's game plan all along? To make her fall in love with him, so she'd break the engagement? Maybe, but he'd outsmarted himself in one way. Josh had been as powerless as she when the situation had flamed out of control. He was right about the awesome attraction between them.

Valentina's heart skipped a beat as she realized his emotions had been as undeniable as hers. If he was serious about dropping his opposition to her marriage, were the other things he said true, also? That he wished he'd met her first? Had Josh come to the same realization she had? Was he in love with her?

The possibility was so heady that she sprang out of bed to pace the floor. What a couple of idiots they were! Out of a desire to shield Warren—whom they both loved in a very special way—they'd refused to admit the truth. But that wasn't fair to Warren, either. She had to cut through all the misunderstandings and tell Josh how she felt about him. One of them had to make the first move, or everybody would suffer.

Valentina was tempted to phone right that minute, but it was now the middle of the night and she was too emotionally exhausted to discuss the situation. Vowing to call him first thing in the morning, she got back into bed and hugged her pillow.

After deciding on a direct course of action, Valentina was so relieved that she slept late the next morning. Josh had already left when she phoned him at home.

She could have called his office, but what she had to say couldn't be said over the telephone. The only solution was to go to his apartment that night after work.

The day seemed to drag on endlessly. Valentina found it difficult to make small talk at lunch. Especially since, for once, Chuck wasn't his usual bubbling self.

"You look like you're dragging your anchor," Valentina observed.

"I am. We closed up the place last night."

She hesitated. "Maybe you should learn to say no to Denise once in a while."

"She was used to a glamorous life before she married me," Chuck said defensively. "It's not very exciting for her here."

"She doesn't have enough to keep her busy. Maybe she should get involved in some kind of community work."

He smiled wryly. "I don't think that's a viable solution for someone like Denise."

"You're probably right." Valentina knew she was fighting a losing battle. Chuck would always find excuses for his wife's selfish behavior.

The long day finally wound to a close. As evening approached, Valentina alternated between euphoria and doubt. What if she was wrong about Josh. It could all be wishful thinking on her part. Would he give up so easily if he really loved her?

Then she remembered his torrid kisses, the urgency of his hardened body holding her close. That could be mere desire, but the regret in his eyes last night told a different story. Josh was bowing out because he thought the situation was hopeless. She had to tell him it wasn't.

* * *

Josh lived in a posh apartment building with all the amenities. A uniformed doorman took Valentina's name and asked if Josh was expecting her.

"Well, no. I, uh, I just dropped by to give him a message."

"I'll ring Mr. Derringer's apartment and see if he's in."

The man's tone was polite, but she could tell he thought she might be one of the unwanted visitors he was paid to discourage. Evidently a lot of women came to see Josh, uninvited. The doorman turned his back and spoke into the house phone in a low voice.

Valentina's relief that Josh was at home was followed by a moment of panic. He didn't know what she'd come to say. Suppose he refused to see her?

The doorman turned back to her. "You can go right up," he said, quieting her fears. "Apartment 12-A."

Josh was waiting in his open doorway when she got off the elevator. He had changed from a business suit to a pair of gray slacks and a navy sport shirt open at the throat. He looked tired and not especially welcoming.

"This is a surprise," he said in a neutral tone.

"Yes, I . . . I suppose it is." Now that she was here, Valentina didn't know how to begin.

"Come in. Would you care for a drink?"

"No—I mean, yes. That would be nice." She didn't want a drink, but it would give them something to do besides stand and stare at each other.

"Go into the living room and sit down. The bar is in the den. I'll be right back."

"I'll come with you." Valentina followed him, glancing around the luxurious rooms they passed through. "You have a lovely apartment. Have you lived here long?"

"About five years." He took an ice tray out of a built-in refrigerator under the bar and emptied the cubes into an ice bucket.

"I suppose it's more convenient than owning a home. You don't have a lot of outdoor maintenance to worry about." She was desperately making small talk, hoping Josh would unbend. He wasn't making a difficult situation any easier.

Handing her a drink, he looked at her levelly. "What's on your mind, Valentina? You didn't come here to see my apartment."

"No, I came because I think we need to have a talk," she began carefully.

"We've said everything we have to say. I gave you my blessing. What more do you want?"

"You haven't really changed your mind. You still think the marriage would be a mistake."

Josh swore under his breath. "What does it take to satisfy you? You're getting what you want. Why do you need my approval?"

"Maybe I'm having second thoughts."

He looked at her sharply. "Isn't that something you should discuss with Warren?"

"I intend to, but I thought you should know, too."

"Why me?"

"Because you're the one who made me realize I wasn't being fair to Warren. He's a wonderful man. I would never want to hurt him."

"I've been telling you that all along. What made it suddenly sink in?"

Valentina bowed her head, looking at the glass clutched tightly in her hands. "I suppose it started with that incident at the center the other night."

"Things like that happen. You're a very beautiful woman, and I'm a normal, healthy male. It isn't anything to get so shaken up over."

A tiny chill touched her spine. "It didn't mean anything to you?"

"Of course it did! I was disgusted with myself. I've never betrayed a friend."

Her heart plunged like a stone. "I haven't, either," she murmured, rising.

"Surely you aren't breaking your engagement over such a minor incident?" he asked incredulously.

"I don't know. I'll have to think about it." She set her drink down and started for the door.

Josh caught her arm. "I should be happy that you've come to your senses, but not for the wrong reason. You didn't betray Warren. What happened was strictly my fault."

"We both know it wasn't," she answered quietly. "I wanted you to kiss me—and then I wanted more than that."

His hand tightened momentarily before he released her arm and moved away. "The sexual attraction between us is very powerful. We've both recognized the fact. That's why I intend to remove any temptation. We're both honorable people."

"I haven't felt like this in a very long time," she said slowly. "I didn't even think I could anymore."

A muscle twitched in his tight jaw. "You haven't been with a man in a long time," he said roughly. "You're all mixed up."

Valentina examined his face without finding what she was seeking. "Perhaps you're right. I'd better go."

"Wait! Are you trying to tell me you think it's more than just sexual attraction?"

"What difference does it make?" she asked hopelessly. "You were right on target. The mere fact that I could feel this way about another man is proof that I shouldn't marry Warren."

Josh's body was taut. "Where does that leave *us*, Valentina?"

She tried to smile. "You must have had a lot of women find you irresistible. Don't worry, I didn't take any of your complimentary remarks seriously."

"I can't think of a one I didn't mean."

"You're very kind." She started toward the door.

Josh blocked the way, his eyes glittering. "I could never express my feelings because of Warren. I even felt guilty about my secret fantasies. But if you've finally realized what a mistake it would be for both of you, that makes a world of difference."

"In what way?" she whispered.

"Darling Valentina." He curled his hand around the nape of her neck and drew her closer. "I've wanted you since the

irst moment I laid eyes on you. You've haunted my wak-
ng hours and tormented my nights.''

"I've been having the same problem," she said with
awning happiness.

His arm curved around her waist, urging her against his
the body. "It's going to be so good with us, angel."

As Josh's head dipped and his lips brushed hers, the front
loor opened and high heels clicked on the marble entry.

"Hello! Is anybody home?" a woman's voice called.

He raised his head with an expression of annoyance.
'Cheryl? Is that you?"

"I knocked, but you must not have heard me, so I used
ny key."

The voice belonged to a very pretty redhead who ap-
eared a moment later. Her flight attendant's uniform
howed off long legs and a lovely figure. She looked star-
led to see Valentina.

"I didn't expect you back until tomorrow," Josh said,
rying to conceal his irritation.

"I had a chance to deadhead back from Miami, so I took
t. You know what Florida is like in the summer," she re-
narked, glancing appraisingly at Valentina.

Josh introduced the two women with remarkable poise.
He didn't even have the grace to look embarrassed, Valen-
ina thought furiously. But perhaps his women were used to
haring him.

"Did you have a nice flight?" he asked Cheryl.

"It was great. I got to be a passenger instead of a combination waitress, bartender and nursemaid. People think a
flight attendant's job is glamorous," she told Valentina.
"They don't realize how much plain hard work is involved."

"I'm sure it can be very difficult," Valentina replied
stiffly. She found it impossible to be as relaxed as the two of
them. All her dreams had been snuffed out.

"Would you like a drink?" Josh asked Cheryl.

"You don't have to be polite." She grinned impishly.

He returned her smile. "Do I score points for trying?"

Valentina couldn't bear the look of intimacy they exchanged. She wasn't sophisticated enough to consider the

situation amusing. "Thank you for the drink," she told Josh formally. "It was nice meeting you, Cheryl."

"You're not leaving?" he asked.

"I never should have come in the first place." Her voice was taut. "I see that now."

His eyes narrowed. "That wasn't the way you felt a few minutes ago."

"You have a knack for making me do things I regret," she flared, not caring what Josh's mistress might think.

He was equally indifferent to Cheryl's presence. "It's difficult for me to shoulder the blame for this one," he drawled. "May I remind you that *you* initiated this meeting."

"Don't worry, it won't happen again!"

"Are you so sure, Valentina?" he asked softly. "You said a lot of interesting things here tonight."

"I was wrong about all of them. I'm just grateful that I found out in time."

"In time for what? You're not still planning to marry Warren?"

"You were very clever," she said bitterly. "You played me like a fish, making me think—well, never mind. I share part of the blame for being so gullible. That tactic last night was masterful—telling me we shouldn't see each other again. You knew that would force me to make a choice. I can't believe I ever thought there was one. Yes, I'm going to marry Warren, and I'll spend the rest of my life being thankful for him."

Without waiting for a response, Valentina ran out of the apartment, holding herself together by sheer force of will. Josh mustn't see how mortally wounded she felt.

Why hadn't she seen him for what he was? A modern-day Casanova who couldn't even be true to the woman he was living with! How convenient for him that her job took her out of town so he was free to romance other women.

Valentina's nails bit into her palms at the realization that she was just one in a long line. If Cheryl hadn't come home so inopportunely, she would have let Josh make love to her.

He hadn't even bothered to try to explain. Although what could he say? The redhead had a key to his apartment! *She* was a cool one, too. Obviously this had happened before. He must be fantastic in bed for her to make such allowances.

Valentina paced the floor distractedly. How had she let Josh slip under her guard? It wasn't as if she didn't know better. Handsome, charming men like him were poison. They had no integrity, no scruples. He wasn't fit to polish Warren's shoes!

Dear Warren. She should have gone to Washington with him, even if the conditions weren't ideal. She not only belonged by his side, that was where she wanted to be. Josh had set out to bewitch her, and he'd almost succeeded. Fortunately she'd come to her senses in time.

When the door slammed behind Valentina, Cheryl whistled. "What brought all that on?"

Josh continued to stare down the hall. After a moment he turned and walked over to splash more scotch into his glass. Deep lines were grooved in his face.

"Nothing to be concerned about," he answered finally.

"Oh, sure! You always look like your pet cat just died."

He shrugged. "Scenes are always unpleasant."

"You're losing your touch, pal. You usually let them down so easy they don't know they've been dumped."

"You're off base," Josh said curtly. "Valentina and I are only friends—at least we used to be. Sort of."

"If you say so. What set your friend off?"

"You did. She obviously jumped to the conclusion that you and I are living together."

"Well, that's easily cleared up. Just explain to her that I live next door and we have each other's keys for convenience's sake. I water your plants, you take my mail when I'm away. That's what I came for. Tell her that."

"Forget it. It isn't that important."

"Don't try to kid me. I know you too well. I've seen your girlfriends come and go without you getting all shook up about it. This time it's different. She really got to you."

He attempted a smile. "I'm as fallible as the next guy. I make mistakes."

"You're being too hard on her. I'd go up in smoke, too, if I thought my boyfriend was cheating on me."

"You don't understand. Valentina has never trusted me."

Cheryl raised an eyebrow. "You never gave her any cause for suspicion? A woman can get downright testy over something a man considers merely a harmless peccadillo."

"Our relationship is very complicated." Josh paced the floor restlessly. "Neither of us wanted to get involved, for reasons I'd rather not go into. We were thrown together a lot, due to circumstances beyond our control, and I guess you could say nature took its course."

"If only sex was involved, you two wouldn't be battling like a couple of foreign countries."

"Okay, so maybe it's more than that for me, but that's all it is with her."

Cheryl couldn't help laughing. "You're upset because she only wants your body? That's a switch."

"It's not funny," he muttered.

"I'm sorry. I couldn't help it." She gave a last snicker. "I'll bet it isn't true, either. A woman doesn't get that upset unless she cares a whole lot about somebody."

"I wish you were right." He sighed.

"There's one sure way to find out. Call her and tell her it was all a misunderstanding."

"She'd probably hang up on me."

"Then *I'll* tell her."

"No!" His jaw set. "There has to be trust for a relationship to work. This isn't the first time Valentina's questioned my motives. I refuse to prove myself over and over again."

"A lot of relationships are rocky in the beginning. Even Romeo and Juliet had their misunderstandings." Cheryl tried to joke him out of his black mood. "At least yours aren't that final."

"They are as far as I'm concerned."

"Oh, Josh, don't be such a dork! Let me call her and set her straight. I feel responsible."

"You needn't. If it hadn't been this, it would have been something else. I don't intend to keep going through these upheavals."

"Are you sure you don't want to reconsider? I've never seen you this disturbed over the breakup of an affair," Cheryl said slowly.

"We weren't having an affair and I'll get over her, so let's just drop the subject. Now, what can I get you to drink?"

"I think I'll skip it. I haven't unpacked yet." She paused in the doorway, looking at the glass in his hand. "Don't drink too much."

"Do I ever?"

"Not that I've noticed."

"Then stop worrying about me. I'm in good shape."

She gazed appraisingly at his tall, broad-shouldered physique. Josh was obviously under stress, but it didn't detract from his attractiveness. What woman could resist that square jaw, those smoldering hazel eyes that were more gold than green? She and Josh had never been romantically involved. They were merely friends of long standing. Even so, Cheryl could feel his physical impact. He'd be a hard act to follow.

"Okay, but if you need a sympathetic ear, I'm right next door," she said.

After Cheryl left, Josh carried his glass and Valentina's into the kitchen. He paused before pouring the contents into the sink, staring at the imprint of lipstick on the rim of hers. Finally he emptied the glass and threw it into the wastebasket under the sink.

"That's how easy it will be," he muttered. "No second thoughts, just out of sight, and out of my life forever."

He didn't look like a man who'd settled all his problems. Josh's eyes were somber as he stood at the window, looking out into darkness.

Chapter Eight

When Warren returned the next day, Valentina's greeting was so fervent that he smiled with pleasure.

"I should go away more often. You must have missed me." He looked at her more closely. "Do you feel all right? You have circles under your eyes."

"It was lonely without you. Next time I'm going along."

"Let's hope there won't be a next time. I've had my fill of bureaucracy for a while."

Valentina smiled. "It goes with the territory. Government officials pledge allegiance to the flag and paperwork."

"And I'm not sure in that order," he agreed. "I don't know what I would have done without Florence."

"Didn't you get a chance to see any of the sights?"

"Only to and from meetings. We did have dinner in a couple of good restaurants." He looked over as his secretary entered the office. "What was the name of the place that served those fantastic crab cakes?"

Valentina didn't hear the answer. She was staring openmouthed at Florence. Her transformation from a drab little wren to a chic, confident woman was nothing short of miraculous. Somewhere between here and Washington she'd adopted all of Valentina's suggestions.

Florence's short, feathery hairdo was very becoming; she'd learned to apply tasteful makeup; and her outfit was fashionable without being far-out. Under a navy sport jacket and a checked skirt that just grazed her knees, she wore a white silk turtleneck pullover. Small gold earrings and a gold coin on a chain around her neck were nice accessories.

She laughed self-consciously at Valentina's incredulity. "I guess you almost didn't recognize me. I went into the beauty shop at the hotel and told them to give me the works."

"Doesn't she look great?" Warren asked. "I almost lost her to a congressman from Indiana. He tried to steal her away from me, and I don't think it was because of her shorthand."

"You know I wouldn't leave you." Florence smiled mischievously. "It would mean a cut in pay."

The change in her appearance had made a difference in her personality, too, Valentina reflected with satisfaction. Florence was more relaxed and open. She might even be fun to be around.

Chuck joined them, looking worn. His frown of concentration vanished when he caught sight of Florence for the first time. Like the others, he complimented her lavishly.

Florence covered her gratification under a crisp manner—although nowhere nearly as brusque as before. "You're all being very nice, but this is still an office. We have a business to run, so let's get back to work."

Warren grinned. "That's the Florence we all know and love."

Chuck put a folder on Warren's desk. It was stamped Top Secret. "This is a progress report on the SX-2 project."

"How's it going?" Warren asked.

Chuck looked uncomfortable. "We're a little behind schedule."

"That's par for the course. Don't worry about it. The sales will be worth a small delay when we finally hit the market with this baby."

"I guess you're right. Well, I'd better get back to my desk."

When Valentina and Warren were alone she said, "What's the matter with Chuck? He isn't his usual sunny self."

"He's been putting in a lot of hours. When this project is finished I intend to give him some time off."

"He does look stressed out. It must be hard to work long hours at the office and then have to take Denise out partying at night. You'd think she'd give him a break."

"Things will ease up when the SX-2 is on the market."

Valentina looked curiously at the manila envelope. "What exactly is it?"

"Do you really want to know?" he asked with a twinkle in his eyes. "You told me computers are the illegitimate offspring of witches and devils."

"I'm convinced of it. Why else would they print mysterious symbols, when I write legitimate words?"

"It couldn't be your typing, could it?" he teased.

"That's right, take their side!"

Warren laughed and kissed her cheek. "How could I be partial to a piece of machinery over a beautiful woman like you?"

"I sometimes get the feeling it's smarter. Tell me what the secret project is, and why it's so hush-hush."

"The SX-2 is an advanced device that foils hackers—people who break into a company's telephone system to make calls all over the world. Telephone fraud accounts for hundreds of thousands of dollars in losses every year. We hope to put an end to that."

"I've read that a clever hacker can find ways to break into even sophisticated systems. How do they do it?"

"Most of them rely on computerized speed dialers that try thousands of phone numbers and passwords. They can usually break a code within a few hours. The SX-2 thwarts most intruders by asking questions in a computerized voice, which confuses the automated dialers."

"It's that simple?" Valentina asked incredulously. "Why didn't somebody else think of that a long time ago?"

"That's only the first defense. If a hacker gets past that hurdle, our artificial intelligence software takes over."

"And does what?"

She listened in fascination as Warren told her in a general way how the system compared calls to user profiles and asked for voice prints. When he saw she was really interested, he gave her a more detailed explanation.

"If it works the way you say it will, all the other systems on the market will be obsolete."

He nodded. "That's why it's top secret. Our competitors are working on similar projects. The first company to perfect the program will corner the market."

"So, poor Chuck is working against the clock. No wonder he looks so haggard."

"You look a little worn yourself." Warren gazed at her with concern. "You've lost weight. Are you working too hard?"

Valentina smiled brightly. "Sitting in front of a typewriter isn't exactly arduous."

"It can be if you don't take enough breaks."

"Stop fussing over me. I'm fine."

He wasn't convinced. "I'm getting worried about you. This isn't the first time you've looked tired. I want you to see a doctor. Maybe you need vitamins."

"I don't need a doctor to prescribe those."

"I want to be sure it's nothing more serious. When was the last time you had a checkup?"

"There's nothing wrong with me," she insisted. "I've just been putting in long hours on the book."

Warren looked skeptical. "We usually quit around six and relax over a cocktail."

"Yes, but while you were gone I worked till all hours of the night," she improvised hastily.

That wasn't why her eyes were shadowed. When she finally managed to fall asleep at night, her dreams were troubled with erotic images of herself and Josh making love. Dream sequences where he drove her almost beyond endurance with his hands, his mouth, his rigid, pulsating body.

She would awaken in the middle of the night, taut with unfulfilled desire. The dreams were so appalling that she was afraid to go back to sleep, lest they recur. It was degrading to still yearn for a man who was nothing but a womanizer.

How could she have mistaken plain, unadulterated sex for love?

"You can't work nonstop!" Warren exclaimed. "Why would you do anything that foolish?"

"We agreed to wait until I finished the book before getting married."

"A couple of weeks one way or the other isn't going to make that much difference."

Her smile was strained. "That's not exactly the remark of an impatient suitor. Are you having second thoughts?"

"My concern is only for you." He cupped her cheek in his palm and gazed at her tenderly. "I want you to take care of yourself."

"You're such a dear man." Valentina turned her head to kiss his palm. "I don't deserve you."

He laughed to avoid showing he was touched. "That will be our little secret. Tonight I want you to knock off early. Go home, take a leisurely bath and get into bed with a good book. No working, you understand?"

"We have tickets to that little theater production in Palo Alto," she reminded him.

"I'll take Florence. She loves the theater almost as much as you do."

"She's entirely too available. I think I've created a monster." Valentina repeated his earlier words to her when she was seeing so much of Josh.

Warren looked at her uncertainly. "Florence has been with me so long she's like an old friend, but if it bothers you, I won't see her outside of the office."

"I was only teasing you. I couldn't be more delighted about her new relationship with all of us. It's so relaxed around here now."

"Florence is a great deal happier, which is gratifying, but you're my main concern. All you've been doing lately is slaving over that book. I haven't even heard you mention the center lately. How is it coming along?"

"Fairly well."

"When will you be ready to open?"

"Soon, I hope. We're just waiting for a final inspection. You know what red tape is like."

Actually, Valentina could only hope that progress was being made. The Foundation's paid staff was handling the final details. She'd laid the groundwork, though. The youth center was an accomplished fact.

"Can't Josh expedite matters?" Warren asked.

"I guess he did as much as he could."

"It isn't like him to wait around meekly. Josh's favorite pastime is lighting fires under bureaucrats." Warren chuckled.

"Everything doesn't always drop into his lap the way he expects!" Valentina said sharply. When Warren looked at her in surprise she added more moderately, "You know what it's like to fight city hall."

"Yes, I suppose so." After a slight pause Warren said, "Josh hasn't been around as much lately. I wonder what's going on."

"He's probably just busy."

"Or involved with a new girlfriend. He left a message on my answering machine saying he couldn't play in the Tuesday-night poker game this week."

"Well, there's your proof." Valentina stood. "I'd better get to work."

Warren continued to speculate. "Whoever it is, she must be something special. Josh doesn't usually let romance get in the way of poker. That's serious stuff." He smiled.

"He'll show up eventually. I'm sure no woman is more important to him than the good-old-boys' club," she said tightly.

"It was only a joke," Warren protested.

"I knew that." She forced herself to smile.

"I wonder if he could really be serious this time," Warren mused. "I think Josh would like to get married and settle down."

"What gave you a bizarre idea like that?"

"Just a feeling I have. Everybody envies the carefree life he leads. They think he has it all, but I know him better than most people. Josh would trade his freedom gladly for a home and children with somebody he loved."

Valentina's lip curled. "At least that's what he wants everyone to believe. You don't know your good friend as well as you think you do. He's laughing all the way to the bedroom."

"That's rather harsh. I thought you'd gotten to like Josh."

"That has nothing to do with it. Women simply see men differently than a man does." She walked to the door. "I'll be in my office if you need me."

Warren stared after her thoughtfully for several minutes before picking up the telephone and dialing Josh's office number.

"You've been neglecting us. Connie thinks you don't like her cooking anymore," Warren joked.

"Tell her I dream about it, but I'm too busy lately to stop for meals."

"It sounds like you're not feeling the recession."

"Or else I have to hustle to make a buck," Josh answered wryly.

"Did you go ahead with that new acquisition you were telling me about?"

"We're still negotiating. These things take time."

"And money. Maybe too much money in this business climate, but I said my piece on that subject. I thought maybe the reason we haven't seen you was because you had a new girlfriend."

"Nothing like that. I'm ready to swear off women."

"I never expected to hear that from *you*. Don't tell me you finally met your match?"

"Believe it! Women," Josh muttered. "They're not happy until they turn your life upside down."

"Sounds serious," Warren remarked.

"It isn't," Josh answered curtly. "Just temporary insanity." He changed the subject abruptly. "What have you been doing with yourself?"

"Why don't you come around and find out?"

"I don't want to wear out my welcome."

"I'll tell you if you do. Haven't we always been straight with each other?"

"Yes, and that's never going to change." Josh's voice was grimly determined.

"Now that that's settled, how about coming over for lunch tomorrow? Connie will cook up a storm."

"I'd like to, but I have meetings all day."

"This weekend, then. Come for a swim and the three of us will go out to dinner afterward."

"I'm tied up on the weekend. Perhaps some other time."

"I understand." Before he could ring off, Warren remarked casually, "Val tells me the center is due to open soon."

"So I hear."

"Aren't you still involved?"

"Oh . . . well, I've been so busy lately that I'm afraid I haven't been much help."

"You and Val haven't been working together?" Warren asked slowly. "I didn't realize that. She never mentioned it."

"There's no reason why she should. Everything's proceeding on schedule—ahead of schedule, actually."

"You two make a good team."

"Yeah, well, don't get any more bright ideas. I've paid off my IOUs into the next century."

"I thought you enjoyed working with youngsters."

"It was an experience I'll never forget," Josh answered with heavy irony. "Just don't ask me to repeat it." Without giving him a chance to reply, he said, "I'm late for a meeting. It was good talking to you, Warren."

The older man cradled the receiver thoughtfully. He was staring out the window when Florence entered the office. She had to speak to him twice to get his attention.

"Is anything wrong?" she asked uncertainly.

After looking at her blankly for a moment, his gaze focused and he sighed. "I was just feeling my age."

"That's a waste of time. There are men a lot younger than you who aren't in as great shape."

"You're good for me, Florence." Warren smiled. "You never let me feel sorry for myself." He reached for the papers she was holding. "Are those the production figures?"

Josh was sitting in the dark, staring out at the moonlit hills, when the doorbell of his apartment rang about eight o'clock. He went to the door reluctantly.

"Did I catch you at a bad time?" Cheryl asked, noticing his frown.

"Not at all. Come on in." He opened the door wider.

"I got a letter from the IRS, and I have no idea what they're talking about. I paid my income tax on time. Will you take a look at it and tell me if I have something to worry about?"

"They rarely send tidings of joy, but come into the den and I'll see if I can figure out what they want." When they reached the den, Josh went around turning on lamps.

"Were you sitting here in the dark?" Cheryl exclaimed.

"What's wrong with that?"

"It's a little peculiar, that's all."

"Okay, so I'm eccentric," he answered irritably.

"I wouldn't say that, but you aren't your usual lovable self tonight. What's eating you, Josh?"

"Nothing." When she simply stared at him skeptically, he said, "I had a rough day at the office."

"Problems?"

He shrugged. "I have a small cash flow problem, but nothing I can't handle."

"Then why aren't you out dancing with some gorgeous cover girl?"

"Because I don't feel like it. Is it so strange to want a little peace and quiet once in a while?"

"My, aren't we grumpy tonight? If you aren't having business reverses, it must be woman trouble. Do you want to tell me about it?"

"No, I don't! I mean, there's nothing to tell."

Josh's set jaw and narrowed eyes warned Cheryl not to pursue the subject. At least not directly. "I've been meaning to ask if you ever straightened things out with that friend of yours," she remarked casually. "What was her name again?"

"I suppose you mean Valentina. No, I haven't spoken to her since that night."

"Too bad. She'd probably get a big laugh out of the mix-up, after you explained it to her. It *was* kind of funny."

"You'll excuse me if I fail to see the humor in the situation."

"You're right. It's always sad to lose a friend, especially over a misunderstanding," Cheryl said ingenuously. "Did you know her long?"

"Not very." Josh jammed his fists into his pockets and paced the room restlessly. "It's Warren's friendship I mind losing. Valentina is Warren Powell's fiancée."

"I *thought* she looked familiar. I saw her picture in the paper. Then you really are only friends!"

"I tried to tell you so."

"Wait a minute." Cheryl's brow puckered. "Why would she be so upset that you were involved with me? Are you two indulging in a little secret hanky-panky? That's not your usual style, Josh." She looked at him disapprovingly.

"You're way off base! Neither of us would do a thing like that."

"If you say so. But what I heard sounded remarkably like a lovers' quarrel."

"We aren't lovers." He hesitated, struggling to find the right words. "I'll admit I'm attracted to her, but that's just chemistry. She's a very beautiful woman."

"You've known a lot of those, but you don't usually sit in the dark brooding over them. At least, I don't think you do."

"I feel guilty because of Warren."

"Why? If you only lusted in your heart." Cheryl smiled.

"Thank God that's all it was," he muttered.

"You might have a lot more on your conscience if I hadn't interrupted," she said slowly. "That's what's bothering you, isn't it?"

"Of course it bothers me! What kind of man would hit on a friend's fiancée?"

"You aren't the only culprit. Nobody forced her to come here. It looks like both of you have a problem."

"Not anymore," Josh said grimly. "I haven't spoken to her since that night."

"That doesn't solve anything. If she was ready to fall into your arms, she shouldn't be marrying another man."

"Don't you think I told her that? I even demonstrated, and now she thinks I was just trying to trick her into breaking the engagement."

"That must have been some demonstration!" Cheryl quickly hid her grin. "At least you can clear up the misconception. Tell her the truth about me."

"It isn't important."

"You'd let them get married, knowing she doesn't love him?"

"She'll make Warren a good wife. He's the only man she trusts." Josh's eyes were bleak.

"It doesn't sound to me like a marriage made in heaven."

"Who are we to judge? They're both getting what they want."

"Where does that leave *you?*"

"I never should have gotten involved in the first place. I'm not God. I can't tell people what to do with their lives."

"Maybe not, but you can clear up the misunderstanding between yourself and Valentina. Otherwise, things are bound to be sticky when the three of you get together."

"That's never going to happen if I can help it," Josh said grimly.

"You don't intend to see Warren again?"

"I'll play poker with him now and then, or we can meet for lunch once in a while."

"You used to hang out there regularly. Don't you think he'll consider it strange when you don't come around anymore?"

"Our lives were bound to change after he got married. You don't honestly think he's going to miss me?" Josh's smile was sardonic.

"I wasn't concerned about *him.*"

"You needn't worry about me, either. Nothing gets me down for long." Without giving her a chance to continue the discussion, he said, "Didn't you want me to look at something? Give me that letter from the IRS and I'll see whether they're warming up a cell for you."

Cheryl realized Josh wasn't going to listen to reason. She went back to her own apartment a short time later, telling herself to mind her own business.

Josh can get all the women he wants, she reasoned. *He'll get over this one.* But if it was only sex between them, they wouldn't be this torn up. It seemed to be a no-win situation, made even worse by his stubbornness. Valentina should be told that he hadn't been trying to manipulate her. If Josh wouldn't tell her, *she* would, and there was no time like the present.

Valentina was trying to read a book when the telephone rang. She picked up the receiver listlessly, then stiffened when she found out who was calling.

"Yes, I remember you," she said coolly, in answer to the other woman's question.

"I thought you might," Cheryl said dryly. "You and I need to have a talk."

"I can't see what we could possibly have to say to each other."

"Let's stop playing games. I know about you and Josh."

"There's nothing to know, and I don't wish to discuss him."

"But *I* do, and you're going to listen."

"There's no need to make a scene. I have no idea what he told you, but you certainly have nothing to fear from me. I don't even like him!"

"He was a little more honest than you're being."

"Whatever he said was a lie," Valentina replied angrily. "There is absolutely nothing between us. He's merely a friend of my fiancé's."

"Is that why you went to Josh's apartment?"

"That was a mistake," Valentina said in a muted voice.

"It very well may have been, but not for the reason you think. Josh and I aren't living together."

"I really couldn't care less."

"You can't even convince *yourself* of that. The plain truth is, I have the apartment next to his. We exchanged keys so we can do neighborly things for each other. Since we're both out a lot, it's also convenient when one or the other of us needs more ice cubes or extra chairs for a party."

"That's a very ingenious explanation. Did he think of it, or did you?" Valentina's scorn was evident.

"Why would I? If we were lovers, why would I try to patch things up between you two?"

In the heat of the moment, that hadn't occurred to Valentina. "If what you're telling me is true, he could have told me," she said slowly.

"You didn't give him much of a chance."

"Maybe not then, but afterward. I never heard from him again. He just let me go on thinking...what I was thinking."

"Men have their pride, too. You accused him without giving him a chance to defend himself. Why should he apologize for something he didn't do?"

"I didn't say he should have apologized, but he certainly could have explained. Anyone would think what I did, given the circumstances."

"Not anyone who knew Josh. He's the nicest guy I've ever met."

"Perhaps I've seen a side of him that you haven't."

"I'm sure you have." Cheryl chuckled.

"I didn't mean it that way!"

"Look, your private lives are none of my business. I'm simply trying to clear up a silly misconception."

"Why should you care?"

"Because I feel responsible. Also, because Josh is miserable about what happened."

"I'm sure you're wrong. He's just angry, and I guess he had reason to be."

"Well, that's a step in the right direction. Why don't you call him and talk it all out?"

"I couldn't do that," Valentina said swiftly. "He'd probably hang up on me."

"You two are something else!" Cheryl exclaimed disgustedly. "That's what he said about you. One of you has to start acting like an adult."

"We can't seem to agree for very long. Something always comes up to set us off. Maybe it's better to leave things the way they are," Valentina said hesitantly.

"Better for whom? The way it stands now, you're costing Josh a friendship he treasures. Do you want that on your conscience?"

"He can still see Warren. I would never try to discourage their friendship."

"How close can it be if you and Josh aren't speaking?"

"We'd be polite to each other if we happened to meet."

"You don't think Warren would notice the strain between you? I'm sure he didn't get where he is by being stupid."

"I doubt if the strain would go away just because I apologized for that one incident," Valentina said somberly. "There are other things you don't know about."

"I can guess—but that's a different problem. You say you always wind up in an argument. Maybe that will change if you talk honestly to each other. I'll bet neither one of you ever has."

"Does Josh know you called me?"

"Lord, no! And you must never tell him. He'd be furious, but I decided it was worth the risk."

"He's very fortunate to have a friend like you who cares so much about him," Valentina said.

"Don't go getting ideas again. We've never been anything more than pals."

"You haven't ever . . ." Valentina paused delicately.

"Noticed what a fantastic specimen he is?" Cheryl laughed. "Of course I have. When I first moved in and found he was my next-door neighbor, I thought I'd really lucked out. This gorgeous man was also charming and had a great sense of humor. A lot of men with his looks are insufferable. All they can talk about is themselves, but Josh seemed more interested in me than himself. He was almost too good to be true."

"I know," Valentina murmured softly.

"I had great plans for us, especially since he was so helpful about pushing furniture around and unpacking cartons for me when I moved in. I thought something would develop between us, until I discovered he was only being neighborly. He didn't feel the same spark. I faced the fact and settled for friendship—which isn't so bad. We have a great relationship. We laugh a lot, and we don't have to pretend with each other. A man like Josh can break your heart if the magic isn't there for both of you."

"I suppose a lot of women can attest to that." Valentina couldn't keep the tinge of bitterness out of her voice.

"That's the prevailing opinion, but there haven't been as many as people think. Josh isn't a womanizer. I really think he'd like to get off the fast track and settle down."

"That's what Warren said, too, but I find it hard to believe."

"If people close to Josh are saying it, perhaps you don't know him as well as you think you do. Has that ever occurred to you? Anyway, it's beside the point. I called to set you straight about Josh and me. Now it's up to you. Call him or don't. I've done everything I can do."

"I . . . I'll think about it. Maybe I will tomorrow. It's too late tonight."

"You could phone him now. I have a feeling he isn't asleep," Cheryl said dryly.

Valentina was filled with a mixture of relief and dismay after talking to Cheryl. No wonder Josh was furious with her. They'd had disagreements in the past, but he'd never given her reason to suspect he was capable of such shameless behavior. Instead of rushing out like an idiot, she should have asked him point-blank why Cheryl had a key to his apartment.

But how could she? It was none of her business what he did in his personal life. Josh had never really given her any indication that he cared about her, except sexually. Anything else was all in her own mind. Valentina saw that now. He didn't even care enough to try to preserve their friendship.

It had been a terrible mistake to go there. If she'd had a chance to say what she'd come to say, she would only have humiliated herself, embarrassed Josh and most important of all, hurt Warren, a wonderful man who deserved better. The only good thing was that Warren would never know about her moment of disloyalty. Valentina vowed to make it up to him for the rest of her life.

Part of her atonement would be to patch things up with Josh. They could never be friends again, that was too much to expect. But if they could manage to be civil to each other, he wouldn't be alienated from Warren. Seeing Josh again, when she'd never expected to go through that torture, would be part of the punishment she deserved.

Taking a deep breath, Valentina reached for the telephone.

Chapter Nine

Josh didn't sound receptive when he answered the telephone. His voice was curt even before he found out who it was.

"I, uh, I hope I didn't wake you," Valentina stammered.

After a nerve-racking moment of silence, he said, "No, I wasn't asleep."

At least he didn't hang up on her, but that was the only comfort she derived. Even though she'd expected hostility, it unnerved her. She didn't know how to begin.

"I know you're there, I can hear you breathing," Josh said sardonically. "Is this an obscene phone call?"

She forced herself to sound unemotional. "I'd like to talk to you, if you're not busy."

"You mean, if I'm not in bed with someone? I sleep alone so rarely."

"I don't blame you for being angry. I called to apologize."

"For what?" he asked roughly.

He wasn't going to make it easy. "For jumping to conclusions about you and Cheryl."

"How do you know you weren't right?"

It was hard to explain without breaking her promise to Cheryl. "I realized I'd been hasty."

"That's a lot of baloney! Cheryl called you, didn't she?"

"Why would you think that?" Valentina hedged.

"Because you'd never have second thoughts in my favor. I'm surprised you believed her, even after she told you the truth."

"Can't you understand?" Valentina pleaded. "You would have thought the same thing if the situation was reversed and a man used his key to my apartment."

"Only if I gave a damn, but you don't, do you, Valentina?" he asked harshly. "So why all the fuss? You're going to marry Warren, isn't that right?"

"Yes," she answered in a barely audible voice.

"For one crazy minute you almost let your heart rule your head. I suppose it was too much to expect that you'd ever really take a chance."

"Was that your game plan all along?" She was overcome with a feeling of hopelessness.

"Since it's what you believe, no apology is necessary. Let's just say, I gambled and lost."

"I suppose you were doing what you thought was right, but how could you be so ruthless? If I *had* fallen in love with you, would you have enjoyed telling me it was all a hoax? I didn't know you could be so cruel."

"I didn't, either. You bring out the worst in me." Josh sighed. "That isn't what I planned at all—which doesn't make my actions any more honorable. You should have left well enough alone, for both our sakes."

"I realize that now."

"Yes, well, no real harm was done."

Did he honestly believe that? Valentina willed herself not to cry. "I'm glad we cleared things up between us, anyway. I know you've missed seeing Warren."

"I'll live through it," he said curtly.

"But it's all right now. You can pick up where you left off."

"Oh, sure! Maybe I should also tell him I coveted his fiancée. Why not let it all hang out?"

"You're overreacting. We didn't actually do anything wrong."

"Through divine providence." Josh's voice was grim. "I don't intend to provoke it any further."

"Nothing will ever happen between us again, I promise you," she said quietly. "I feel as guilty as you do—perhaps guiltier because I came between you and Warren. He misses you. He wonders why he hardly ever hears from you."

"I know. He called me."

"What did you tell him?"

"That I've been busy. It's the truth."

"You can't use that excuse forever. Warren will think you're miffed about something."

"What do you suggest? That we resume our carefree weekends around the pool?"

"Only for one Sunday. After that I'll find some excuse not to be there, and you two can go back to your old relationship. Warren just needs to be reassured that I'm not the reason you're staying away."

"Sounds like a really fun afternoon," Josh remarked with heavy sarcasm.

"It won't be easy for me, either, but we both care deeply about him. I don't want Warren to suffer for my mistake. It's up to you, though. If you think you'd be too uncomfortable around me, perhaps you can think of some other way to salvage your friendship. I know Warren would appreciate it."

Josh hesitated for a moment. "Let me think about it."

"Certainly." After an awkward pause she said, "Well . . . maybe I'll be seeing you."

Josh telephoned Warren a few days later. "Are you doing anything Sunday afternoon?" he asked.

"That's our day to lie around the pool," Warren replied. "Will you join us?"

"I was hoping you'd ask."

"Since when do you need an invitation? Come early and we'll have lunch."

"I was hoping you'd say that, too."

Warren was smiling when he hung up the receiver. "That was Josh," he told Valentina, who had just entered his office. "He's coming over on Sunday."

Her hands gripped the papers she was carrying, but outwardly she remained serene. "That's nice."

Warren looked at her closely. "You'll be here, won't you?"

"Of course. Why wouldn't I be?"

"I don't know. I thought . . . well, never mind. It will be like old times. I've missed the guy."

"It hasn't been that long," Valentina said lightly.

"You're right, I'm being selfish. After Marian died he went out of his way to be there for me, but Josh has his own life to live."

"I'm sure you'll always have a place in it. You shouldn't expect him to come over here all the time, though," she remarked in a casual tone. "You two should do more guy things together."

"I guess you're right. You have a tendency to get into a rut when you get older."

"Let's not have any of that kind of talk. You're in the prime of life," Valentina said affectionately.

He looked at her thoughtfully. "Sometimes I think I'm not being fair to you. I've traveled the whole nightclub circuit and gone to all the fancy parties. The social whirl doesn't hold any allure for me. I'm content now to go out for a quiet dinner and some good conversation. But you're still young. You should be doing all those things."

"I'm perfectly happy," she assured him. "Have I ever complained?"

"No, but I wouldn't want you to wake up a few years from now and feel cheated. I'd understand if you were having a few doubts."

"*I* wouldn't. You're the best thing that ever happened to me. I never expected to find anyone like you."

A slight frown creased his forehead. "You're a very beautiful young woman. A lot of men must have lost their heads over you. It's unusual that you never fell in love with any of them."

"We had this conversation when you asked me to marry you," she said evenly. "What I feel for you is more lasting than mere sexual attraction. Which doesn't mean I don't find you attractive," she was quick to add. Her gaze sharpened. "Why did you bring it up now? Are *you* having second thoughts?"

"Only on your behalf. I want you to be happy."

That was so typical of Warren. "I will be if I can make *you* happy," she answered tenderly.

After Valentina left him, Warren shuffled aimlessly through the manuscript pages she'd placed on his desk. He was staring at them blankly when Florence entered the office.

"You've always told me the truth," he said abruptly. "Do you think I'm an old fool?"

"You're not old." She grinned impishly.

"But you do think I'm a fool."

"No, of course not! I was trying to make a joke, but I'm not very good at it yet."

He stared at her appraisingly. Florence had on a red linen sheath that showed off her trim figure in an understated way. She wore nail polish now and bright lipstick that accentuated her generous mouth.

"You're a damned attractive woman, Florence. One of these days some man is going to come along and take you away from me."

She laughed self-consciously. "I don't think there's any danger of that at my age."

"If I'm not old, you certainly aren't."

"It's different with men. They're considered more desirable as they grow older. Women aren't. We're living in a youth-oriented society."

"Youth is overrated," he said dismissively. "It's the person who counts, and what you have in common with each other."

"I suppose you're right." Florence's eyes dropped. "I have those charts you asked for."

Warren's expression was sober as he watched her leave the room. Then the telephone rang and he became engrossed in business.

Valentina's nerves were wound tightly that Sunday at Warren's house. Her heart rate speeded up even more when Josh arrived. He looked as lean and handsome as ever, she thought despairingly. The breeze ruffled his thick dark hair as he moved with easy grace across the patio. He was smiling, but she couldn't see his eyes. They were hidden behind dark glasses.

"Welcome, stranger," Warren called. "It's been a while."

"Nothing's changed." Josh's white teeth showed in his tanned face. "You're still lying on the same chaise."

Warren chuckled. "Val already pointed that out. She told me I'm in a rut."

"You were the one who said that," she protested. "I only said you should see more of your men friends."

"Do you think she's trying to get rid of me?" Warren joked.

"I doubt it very seriously," Josh answered. "How's it going, Valentina?"

"Couldn't be better." Her tone was light, but her fingernails were making crescent marks in her palms. She hadn't realized it was going to be this hard to make small talk with him.

"How about a drink before lunch?" Warren asked.

"Sounds good to me. I'll fix them," Josh offered.

"Just ginger ale for me," Valentina said.

"I know," Josh answered. "Drinking in the daytime makes you sleepy."

"You have a good memory," she remarked.

His jaw set. "Sometimes it can be a curse." Turning immediately to Warren, he said, "You should have a bar in the pool house."

"I thought *I* was the old man around here. How lazy can you get?" After Josh had gone into the house, Warren said to Valentina, "Does Josh look thinner to you?"

"I really didn't notice."

"It's probably my imagination, but I worry about him. I hope he hasn't gotten himself too involved."

"I don't know what you mean," she said carefully.

"This acquisition he has his heart set on. I think it's too risky."

"I wouldn't know anything about that. The electronics industry is a complete mystery to me. I don't know a floppy disk from a hard drive."

"The basic rules apply to any business. I'm afraid Josh is overextending himself." After a moment Warren's frown vanished. "But what the heck? When I was his age, I wanted to be king of the mountain, too. Josh is clever. Even if he does get into a tight spot, he'll find some way to save his neck."

"I'm sure you're right," Valentina murmured.

Her tension increased when Josh returned with the drinks. They both tried hard to banter together the way they used to, but it sounded forced. She was happy when it was time to go inside and bring lunch out.

"I'd help, but age has its privilege," Warren declared.

"What's this fixation you have with age all of a sudden?" Josh asked.

"Maybe I'm feeling mine." Warren gazed at the younger man's trim physique.

"Tell him that's nonsense," Valentina said. "He won't believe me."

Josh took off his sunglasses. Their eyes met for a moment before he turned to Warren. "You have everything a man could ever want, so stop talking like a jackass."

"You're not supposed to insult your host," Warren joked.

Josh's taut body relaxed. "You call that an insult? How about what you called me when I bluffed you out of that big pot at the last poker game?"

"That reminds me. Can we count on you next Tuesday night?"

"I wouldn't miss it. I could use an infusion of cash right now," Josh said.

"Talk about overconfidence! The boys are just waiting to take you to the cleaners."

Valentina went into the house, feeling a little better. Today was as difficult as she'd expected it to be, but the important thing was that Warren and Josh were back to normal. From now on, she would invent things she had to do on Sundays, and Josh would get tickets to sporting events for just himself and Warren. Gradually it would seem normal to exclude her. And they'd all live happily ever after, she thought sardonically.

Lunch was more relaxing. The men talked about the coming football season and the Forty Niners' chances. Valentina enjoyed football, but she pretended disinterest. She closed her eyes, partly so she wouldn't have to look at Josh.

When the sun became uncomfortably warm, they decided to go swimming. Warren was already in bathing trunks, and Josh had his on under his clothes, but Valentina was wearing the halter-neck sundress she'd driven over in. She went into the cabana to change.

When she started to untie the bow at the back of her neck, it knotted somehow. After trying without success to untangle it, she was forced to go outside for help.

The men were still lying where she'd left them, except that Josh had stripped down to his bathing trunks. Valentina sat on the edge of Warren's chaise and lifted her long hair.

"Will you untie me? I can't get out of this thing."

He fumbled ineffectually for a few moments. "How did you get this knot so tight?"

"Who knows? A natural talent for clumsiness, I guess."

"I can't loosen it. Let Josh try."

"Maybe I'll just cut the straps," she said swiftly.

"You might have to, but at least let him take a whack at it."

Valentina reluctantly went over to Josh's chaise and sat down with her back to him. When his hands touched her neck she arched her body as if he'd dropped an ice cube down her back.

"Hold still, or it will take longer," he ordered grimly.

The feeling of his hands on her neck and his warm breath on her sensitized skin was torture. She was painfully aware of his lithe, almost nude body just inches from her own.

When her nerves were at the screaming point, the halter loosened slightly.

"There, I've almost got it," he said.

"Great! I can undo it now."

She started to get up, but Josh's arm snaked around her waist, pulling her against him. "Let me finish," he grated. "You'll only get it knotted again, and I don't want to spend all day doing this."

After she remained still, Josh mercifully removed his arm from around her waist. Valentina sat rigidly so their bodies wouldn't touch again. The fleeting contact had been incendiary.

"Okay, that does it," he said.

As the straps loosened, Josh's hand slid gently over her shoulder. Not on purpose, she was sure, but it was agony nonetheless. Her cheeks were flushed as she held her dress in front and got up without looking at him.

Warren was watching them with an enigmatic expression. "Josh is a good man to have around, isn't he?"

Valentina didn't answer directly. "I really did a number on myself." She started to walk toward the cabana. "It will only take me a couple of minutes to change, but you two don't have to wait for me. I'll see you in the pool."

During the afternoon, Warren brought up the subject of the youth center. "Are you planning any kind of festivities for the grand opening?"

"We haven't thought of it," Valentina said.

"It's a good way to get the goodwill of the neighborhood."

"And a chance for everybody, including the kids, to see the facilities," Josh agreed. "They'll flock to the place once they find out what we have to offer."

"I think it's a wonderful idea," she said excitedly. "We can decorate the place with balloons and have free food. Maybe hot dogs and pizza. Those always go over big with kids."

"What, no elegant buffet?" Josh teased.

"Don't remind me!" Valentina laughed. "I learned that lesson the hard way." She told Warren about the last night at camp when the buffet dinner met with less than enthusiasm. "I should have known better."

"It wasn't your fault," Josh said. "I thought it was a great idea, too."

"Remember what Gary said the beef Stroganoff looked like?"

"I'd prefer not to." Josh chuckled. "It used to be one of my favorites, but I might never be able to eat it again."

"We can't expect to turn them into gourmets with one dinner, but we did get through to them in more important ways."

"And now we'll have a chance to keep the momentum going."

"I'd like to see this center you're so high on," Warren commented.

"Your money paid for it," Josh said. "Get Valentina to show you around. This is her project."

"Are you disassociating yourself from it?"

"I'll be around if any problems arise," Josh answered casually. "But most of the work is done. It doesn't take two people from here on."

"I see," Warren murmured.

It was late afternoon when Warren asked where they wanted to go for dinner.

"Will you give me a rain check?" Josh answered. "I have an early-morning budget meeting and I need to go over some figures." He left soon after that.

Valentina was both relieved and depressed. This was the last Sunday they'd spend together.

"Would you mind if we made this an early evening, too?" Warren asked when they were alone. "I haven't done anything but lie around all day, but for some reason I'm rather tired."

"Me, too," she answered. "It must be the sun. That always takes it out of me. Where would you like to have dinner?"

"I'll leave that up to you."

"How about the Granada? We won't tell Connie we ate somebody else's Mexican food." Valentina grinned.

Warren made a wry face. "Not tonight. To tell the truth, my stomach is sort of upset."

Valentina was immediately concerned. "We don't have to go out. I'll fix you something light like an omelet, or maybe some soup."

"That isn't necessary. I'm all right. I just don't feel like any spicy food."

"You're staying right here," she said firmly. "Why don't you take a shower and get into your pajamas while I'm fixing dinner?"

"I'm not sick," he protested mildly. "I just feel a little under the weather."

"That's why you should eat lightly and go to bed early. You're always fussing over *me*. Let me take care of *you* for a change."

"That's really sweet."

"I care a lot about you."

"I know you do, my dear." He smoothed her hair fondly. "All right, you win. It might be nice to be pampered for a little while."

"I can't think of anyone who deserves it more." She leaned down and kissed him.

An unfamiliar car was parked in Warren's driveway when Valentina arrived the next morning. She was only mildly interested until she went inside and discovered it belonged to Warren's doctor.

"What happened?" she asked sharply. "He was fine when I left here last night."

Florence's face was drawn. "He has a high fever. I could tell something was wrong, so I insisted on calling the doctor, although he kept saying it wasn't necessary."

"You did the right thing." Valentina hurried down the hall to Warren's bedroom.

He was sitting up in bed while the doctor took his pulse. Warren gave her a slightly wan smile. "Everybody's making a big fuss over nothing."

"A hundred and two temperature in an adult is not to be taken lightly," the doctor said. "I think you should go to the hospital."

Valentina paled, but Warren said, "So you can justify those fat bills you send me? I'll let you win at poker instead. Jim is one of my card-playing buddies," he explained to her before introducing the man as Dr. James Copeland.

"What's the matter with him, Doctor?" she asked.

"I have the flu," Warren answered for him. "Can you imagine going to the hospital for a commonplace thing like that?"

"Will you show me where I can wash my hands?" the doctor asked Valentina.

"You can use my bathroom," Warren said.

Jim ignored the suggestion and started for the door, beckoning her with an imperceptible movement of his head. She followed him with apprehension.

When they had moved down the hall a short way he said, "Warren has always been as stubborn as a mule. Maybe you can convince him. I honestly feel he should be in the hospital."

"Is there something you're not telling us? Warren's right. People don't usually need to be hospitalized for the flu."

"This is a particularly virulent strain. It's related to the kind that caused an epidemic in the twenties."

Valentina's heart lurched. "My grandmother used to talk about that. A lot of people died from it."

"That was before antibiotics and all the other drugs we have now," he said soothingly. "I don't mean that Warren is seriously ill, but children and older people are always at greater risk." The doctor paused, looking momentarily uncomfortable. "Not that Warren is old, by any means. It's just that it's always wise to take precautions."

"Then of course he should go!" she exclaimed.

"Good. Now *you* convince him."

Warren resisted valiantly, but he was no match for the three of them. Florence added her voice to the rest.

Warren was given the VIP treatment at the hospital. Except for the high hospital bed, his room looked more like a suite in a luxury hotel. One end of the long room was furnished as a sitting area, with a couch and several comfortable chairs. Cheerful printed draperies framed the windows and the walls were painted a neutral cream, instead of the usual depressing hospital color of green or ocher.

"This is lovely," Valentina commented. "You'll be as comfortable as you are at home."

"That sounds like you expect me to be here for a couple of weeks," Warren growled. "I agreed to this nonsense to keep you all quiet, but I'm only staying overnight."

"You're sending your blood pressure sky-high," Jim commented. "Calm down and let the nurses do their job."

Several young women in white uniforms surrounded the bed. One placed a thermometer in Warren's mouth and took his pulse. A second wrapped a wide black cuff around his upper arm to monitor his blood pressure, while another nurse stood by with a tray filled with instruments and little glass vials.

Warren stared at her irritably. "Will you kindly tell these young ladies that I'm not here for open-heart surgery," he mumbled.

"Keep your mouth closed so she can take your temperature," Jim answered.

After one of the nurses had recorded his vital signs on a chart, she brought it over and showed it to the doctor.

"Prepare an IV and start him on tetromonacine every three hours around the clock," he said in a low voice.

Valentina was gripped by fear, but she kept her voice equally low. "Does he have something besides the flu?"

Instead of answering, Jim called to Warren, "We're going to step out into the hall until the nurses finish with you."

When they were outside in the corridor, Valentina demanded, "Tell me what's wrong. It's serious, isn't it?"

"His temperature is up a little bit, but I wouldn't call that critical."

"More than a hundred and two?" she gasped.

"Somewhat," he answered noncommittally. "But we have ways to bring it down. That's why I wanted him here in the hospital."

"How could it have gone up in such a short time?"

"A high fever is one of the characteristics of this strain of influenza. Try not to worry. Why don't you go home now and come back this evening? He'll probably be a lot more comfortable by then."

"Are you kidding? I'm not leaving here until I know he's all right."

"Everybody gives me an argument. You're as bad as Warren," he joked. "Okay, stick around, but prepare yourself for a long, boring day."

"I intend to sleep here tonight. Will you tell the nurses it's all right?"

After a look at her determined face, Jim said, "I suppose I can get you a room."

"Don't bother. I'll sleep on the couch." Before he could argue, she asked, "Where are the pay phones?"

"There's a telephone in Warren's room."

"I'd rather use a public phone where he can't hear me. I have to call Florence. I know she's worried sick."

"Tell her to calm down, too. I'm not going to let anything happen to Warren. The boys in the poker club would never forgive me."

Valentina did her best to reassure Florence, despite her own misgivings. Then she went back to Warren's room.

It was a long, frightening afternoon. He looked a lot sicker than he had at home, partly because of the shapeless hospital gown and the plastic tube in his arm. The nurse explained that it was a harmless solution to prevent him from dehydrating, but Valentina wasn't convinced that anyone was telling her the truth.

Warren slept a good part of the day, due to a combination of high fever and medication. Valentina alternated between staring out the window and hovering over his bed to be sure he was still breathing.

He awoke toward evening and scolded her when he found out what time it was. "Have you been here all day? That's nonsensical."

"I wanted to be sure you didn't flirt with any of the pretty nurses." She smiled, holding on to his hand.

"You probably didn't have anything to eat, either. I want you to go home and have a nice hot dinner."

"I wouldn't get that at home. You know I'm a terrible cook. I thought I'd eat here with you."

"Nobody eats hospital food if they don't have to. There's a law against cruel and inhuman punishment."

"Don't knock it till you've tried it." Valentina laughed. "For someone who's a pussycat around the office, you're a terrible patient."

He smiled gamely. "If you don't assert yourself right from the beginning, they walk all over you."

Dr. Copeland entered the room and walked over to the bed. "How do you feel?"

"Worse than I did at home," Warren answered testily.

"What did you expect? Hospitals are filled with sick people." Jim pulled a stethoscope out of his pocket and listened to his patient's chest.

"Well, what's the verdict?" Warren demanded.

"Your heart's beating. That's a good sign."

"Just what I need," Warren said disgustedly. "A doctor who thinks he's a stand-up comic."

Valentina would have been encouraged by their banter, except that Warren didn't look well. His face was drawn, and his eyes were still bright with fever. She also detected concern under Jim's relaxed manner.

Florence appeared in the doorway and paused hesitantly. She was carrying a small overnight case. "Is it all right to come in?"

"Of course. I hope you have some pajamas in that suitcase," Warren said. "No grown man should have to sleep in a gown that's open down the back."

Jim grinned. "You could turn it around, but the nurses might think you were a flasher."

"I'll bring you some pajamas tomorrow," Florence promised. "I didn't know they'd let you wear your own. I just brought a nightgown and a few other things for Valentina."

"I'm staying here with you tonight, and I don't want to hear any arguments," Valentina stated.

That didn't stop Warren. He was even more vocal when he heard she was sleeping on the couch in his room.

"You *must* be sick," Jim joked. "Any healthy man would be thrilled to have a beautiful woman spend the night with him. Why don't you two ladies step outside while I examine Mr. Congeniality?"

"How is he, really?" Florence asked as they walked down the hallway.

"I honestly don't know. I think Jim is concerned, but he doesn't want us to see it."

"Is there anything I can do? Would you like me to come in tomorrow and sit with him while you go home for a few hours?"

"No, thanks. I don't want to leave him."

Florence hesitated for an instant. "I guess this is as good a time as any to say I'm sorry for misjudging you. I didn't think you really loved him."

Valentina glanced away. "I care very deeply for Warren. I'd do anything for him."

"Yes." Florence sighed heavily. "So would I."

"I'm sorry," Valentina said gently.

The two women gazed at each other for a moment in unspoken understanding. Florence broke the silence. "I brought you one of my nightgowns and some fresh underwear and makeup."

"That was very thoughtful of you."

Florence forced a smile. "Oh, well, it's thanks to you that I have any makeup to bring."

Warren was very restless during the night. The nurses were in and out of his room regularly. Valentina snatched a catnap here and there, but for the most part she was awake all night.

The next day his fever went down slightly, but he still looked and felt terrible. It wasn't until the third day that he showed marked improvement.

"You can go home now," he told Valentina. "You must be sicker of this place than I am."

"How can you complain?" Her smile was brilliant with relief, in spite of her fatigue. "You had nurses waiting on you around the clock, and your friends bought out every florist shop in town."

The large room was crammed with floral arrangements, plants and clusters of balloons. So many bouquets had arrived that Warren sent dozens of them to the children's ward.

"I appreciate the good wishes, but it's like getting a preview of your own funeral," he said dryly.

"I doubt if there will be any balloons." She laughed.

Warren shuffled through the multitude of cards on the nightstand. "I didn't see anything here from Josh, and he hasn't phoned, either. That isn't like him."

"No, it isn't." Valentina was as puzzled as he.

"You don't think he could be sick, too?"

"It would be quite a coincidence. Perhaps he hasn't heard you're in the hospital."

"That could be it." Warren sounded justifiably doubtful, since everyone else in the industry seemed to know.

"I think I'll go home for a few hours, if you don't mind. Florence was darling to lend me some blouses and things, but I'd like to change into my own clothes. I'll be back this afternoon."

"You don't have to come back," he said firmly. "You must be exhausted. Go home and stay there. Get a good night's sleep for once. You certainly didn't get any here."

"I can sleep any old time." She leaned down and kissed him. "I'll see you later."

Valentina fully expected to change clothes, pack a bag and return to the hospital immediately. Lying down on the bed to rest for just a few minutes was a mistake. She fell asleep for several hours. By the time she drove back to the hospital it was early evening.

When she rushed into Warren's room, Josh and Florence were there.

"You were right about Josh," Warren told her happily. "He didn't know I was in the hospital."

"I had to go out of town," Josh explained. "I was shocked when I came home and heard what happened. You were fine on Sunday." He looked at the older man with a perplexed frown.

"He wasn't feeling well, but he didn't tell us," Valentina said. "If he'd said something, we could have called the doctor right then. I'm so aggravated with him!"

"What were you trying to be, macho man?" Josh demanded.

"Stop ganging up on me. In case you two haven't noticed, I'm sick," Warren complained. "Defend me, Florence."

She smiled at him before turning to the others with an expression of mock severity. "If you don't stop harassing the patient, you'll have to leave."

"That's an excellent idea," Warren said. "Josh, I want you to take Valentina out to dinner. She's been stuck here for three whole days, and I know she hasn't had a decent meal."

"You're exaggerating," she said swiftly. "I just got back."

"You went home for only a few hours," he said. "And don't tell me you've been eating regularly. I don't want to hear any arguments. Let Josh take you out to dinner. Florence will stay here and keep me company, won't you?" he asked her.

"I'll be happy to." She looked delighted.

"Is it all right with you, Josh?" Warren asked belatedly.

"If Valentina would like to go," Josh answered slowly. "She probably doesn't want to leave you."

"I insist on it. Get moving, you two. I want to talk to Florence about what's been going on at the office. In spite of that paranoid doctor, I still have a business to run."

"You shouldn't be thinking about business yet," Valentina protested weakly, aware that she was fighting a losing battle.

He waved a dismissive hand at her and turned to the other woman. "Bring me up to date on the SX-2 project."

With a despairing glance at Josh, Valentina preceded him out of the room.

Chapter Ten

When Valentina and Josh were safely out of Warren's hearing, she said, "We don't have to go to dinner. I'll just grab a bite somewhere. He'll never know the difference."

"I'm not so sure." Josh smiled. "Warren is very astute."

"Sometimes I wonder." She sighed.

"Well, it's no big deal. Neither of us has had dinner, so we might as well have it together."

"I suppose so." She didn't want to seem to overreact.

They agreed on a popular Italian restaurant near the hospital, noted for good food. When she smelled the appetizing aromas, Valentina found she was hungry for the first time in days.

"Shall we have a drink first?" Josh asked.

"I'd better just have a glass of wine. I don't know what a stronger drink might do to me. I haven't had anything to eat today."

"Are you afraid I might take advantage of you?" he teased.

She forced herself to match his light tone. "Maybe it would be the other way around."

Josh's face sobered as he gazed at her. Valentina's blue eyes were shadowed and her tawny hair was windblown, but she was breathtakingly lovely.

He changed the subject deliberately. "You must have had a rough week."

"I was so worried about Warren. The doctor didn't want to scare me, but I know a temperature that high is dangerous."

"Especially in an older person." Josh nodded. "I didn't mean to imply that Warren is old," he added quickly. "Anybody would be at risk with that much fever."

"I knew what you meant," she murmured.

"I wish I'd been here. What a rotten time to be out of town!"

"He had the finest care. There wasn't anything you could have done."

"I could have been here to hold your hand, if nothing else."

That would only have been an added distraction. "Was your trip business or pleasure?" she asked.

"Business. I flew to Southern California to complete an acquisition I'm planning."

"The one Warren doesn't approve of?"

Josh smiled. "Sometimes he's like an overly protective father."

"He's proud of your success. He doesn't want you to take chances with it."

"You have to take risks in order to grow. Warren is speculating on the new project he's developing. From what I hear, he's pouring a fortune into it."

"I don't think it's speculative. I'm not very knowledgeable about electronics, but it seems to me that every company would buy it—certainly every large business. There may even be a market in the private sector."

"The marketplace is already crowded with personal computers."

Valentina shook her head. "The SX-2 isn't merely an advanced model, it's a security system."

"Those are in the stores, too. Consumers can buy every thing from a simple surge protector to a complicated tech nique to screen out viruses."

"This is a lot more important. It's a device to eliminate hacker rip-offs. Other people may be making them, but the SX-2 is the first almost foolproof antihacker system."

"*Almost* foolproof," he said skeptically. "Hackers al ways find a way to breach security eventually."

"Not this one. It compares calls to user profiles and ask for a voice print if it notices something out of the ordi nary."

"That's a novel concept. They could all be stored i memory," Josh said thoughtfully. "What does it do if i detects someone rummaging through the phone system What response time does it have?"

She wrinkled her brow in an effort to remember. "I thin it's something like ten minutes, at the most. First the devic automatically calls managers to tell them the company i under attack. If it can't reach any of the people on its list, i shuts off access to the phones."

"Can the voice print match up a single word, or does i require a phrase?"

She answered Josh's probing questions to the best of he ability. When she didn't know the answer, he speculate about the various methods that could be used. Valentina wa impressed with his expertise. But Josh was good at every thing, she thought wistfully.

"Damned ingenious," he said finally. "I wish I'd though of it. Warren's going to make more millions."

Valentina was stuck by belated caution. "Maybe shouldn't have told you. This is very top secret."

"It's safe with me. I couldn't be happier for him. Eve though Warren needs a few more million like I need a hea cold." Josh grinned.

"I couldn't resist showing off," she said ruefully. "H explained it to me in detail, and I was so proud of myself fo understanding. I'm usually hopeless when it comes to elec tronics."

"You're too hard on yourself. I'm sure you could mee any challenge if you really wanted to."

"You're just being polite."

"No, I'm not. I was thinking about the camping trip that could have turned into a disaster. You were equal to *that* challenge."

"You didn't expect me to last the week. Admit it."

"Not when we were discussing it at Warren's that day. I think he had his doubts, too. That's why he wouldn't let us wager breakfast in bed."

"It was a silly bet, anyway. If I did eat breakfast, I wouldn't want it served to me in bed."

"Don't knock what you haven't tried," Josh said softly.

It was something she'd only read about in romantic novels—and dismissed as probably being overrated. But Josh's honeyed voice suggested otherwise. Would he kiss her awake, or would he caress her sleep-warmed body until she held out her arms to him?

She hoped Josh didn't notice the rush of color to her cheeks. "The entire bet was academic from the beginning. We're both too competitive to ever give an inch."

"You're right. It was a no-win situation from the beginning," Josh said flatly. "Would you care for more coffee?"

"No, thanks. I'd really like to get back to the hospital."

"I'll get the check." Josh signaled for the waiter.

Valentina searched for something to break the awkward silence that fell. "Thank you for dinner," she said finally. "I hope I didn't spoil any of your plans."

"Not at all. I enjoyed talking to you," he said politely.

She gave him a lopsided smile. "I won't say let's do it again, but I enjoyed myself, too. It was good to get away from the hospital. I guess these last three days were more grueling than I realized."

"I can imagine. Warren said you insisted on sleeping in his room."

"I wanted to be there so he'd see a familiar face in case he awoke in the middle of the night. People can feel abandoned in a hospital, even when they're getting excellent care."

"I understand." The waiter brought Josh's change. After leaving some bills on the tray, Josh said to her, "Shall we go?"

He left her off at the entrance to the hospital.

"Aren't you coming in?" Valentina asked.

"No, I don't want to tire Warren out. Two visitors are enough at one time, and I'm sure Florence is still there."

"Well . . . it was nice seeing you," she said tentatively.

"You, too. Tell Warren I'll stop by tomorrow." He waited patiently for her to get out, gazing at her without emotion.

Valentina walked slowly up the path to the front door, trying to figure Josh out. His emotions were a mystery to her, as always.

This was assuredly the last time they'd ever spend alone together. She'd said that before, but they both knew their relationship had to end. It didn't seem to bother Josh. There had been some bittersweet moments during dinner when he'd tantalized both of them with what might have been, yet you'd never know it by the way he said goodbye.

Well, it didn't matter now. It was just as well that he'd accepted the situation the way she had.

Warren recovered rapidly from then on, although the doctor insisted on keeping him in the hospital for another couple of days. Valentina spent all day there, but she felt confident enough now to go home at night.

Things returned to normal after Warren was allowed to go home. The only problem was getting him to take it easy. He was filled with energy after his stay in bed, unlike the people around him.

Chuck looked worn, Florence wasn't her usual efficient self, and Valentina was experiencing the fatigue that often followed a period of high tension. She slept later and sometimes didn't show up at Warren's until mid-morning.

It was around ten-thirty a couple of weeks later that she arrived to find the driveway clogged with cars. Warren must have called a meeting of all his high-level people, she decided with a tinge of irritation. He shouldn't be pressuring himself this way.

The door to his office was closed, which was unusual. Connie came down the hall as Valentina was trying to decide whether to knock and tell Warren she was there, or wait until the meeting was over. The housekeeper was wheeling a tea cart that held a coffee urn and some cups and saucers.

"What's going on, Connie? Mr. Powell didn't tell me he was scheduling a meeting for today. I guess he knew I'd try to talk him out of it." Valentina smiled.

"This isn't an ordinary meeting. I don't know what happened, but some of those men in there are detectives."

"Are you sure? What would detectives be doing here?"

"That's what I'd like to know, but nobody told me anything. About an hour ago the phones began to ring like crazy, and Miss Florence went rushing into Mr. Powell's office and closed the door. Then all these men started to arrive."

"But how do you know they're detectives?"

"Not all of them are. Some are people who work for Mr. Powell. I know about the others because Miss Florence said when the detectives got here I should ask them to show their badges and then send them right in."

"What on earth!" Valentina exclaimed. "When you take the coffee in, would you tell Florence I'd like to speak to her for a minute?"

Florence looked distracted when she came out into the hall a few moments later.

"What's wrong?" Valentina asked apprehensively. "Why are the police here? Is Warren all right?"

"It's a catastrophe! Someone pirated the plans for the SX-2 project. Draeger Software Systems hit the market with it this morning. Their stock is going through the roof."

"I don't understand. You mean, they perfected it before we did?"

"They stole it from us," Florence said succinctly.

"That's terrible! Who would do such a thing?"

"Anyone who wanted to make a lot of money fast. Draeger must have paid a fortune for the information."

"But how could anybody get away with it? Those plans were guarded like the crown jewels. Only a handful of people had access to them."

Florence shrugged. "We're in a high-tech business. That's what makes industrial espionage so difficult to combat."

"I hope they catch whoever is responsible and put him away for a very long time!"

"Even if they do, the damage has already been done. All that work down the drain." Florence suddenly looked tired. "I have to get back inside."

Poor Warren, Valentina thought as she went into her office. It wasn't the money so much as the feeling of being betrayed. It couldn't have been any of the people who worked for him, though. Warren was legendary in the industry for the loyalty of his employees. They hardly ever left him.

Ordinarily, Chuck would have been the logical suspect. He was in charge of the entire project. But Chuck was like a member of the family. He had a bright future with the company, and he admired and respected Warren. Could he have inadvertently told Denise too much about the SX-2, maybe even showed her the plans? Denise would have no compunction about selling her own mother for a lot less than the amount involved.

While that was the harsh truth, Denise couldn't be considered a prime suspect since she never listened to anything Chuck said, especially about business. If he'd ever tried to talk to her about his job, she'd have cut him off fast. Denise wouldn't have realized Chuck had secret information that could have made her rich, Valentina reflected sardonically.

A chilling thought occurred to her. Chuck wasn't the only one with inside information. Valentina flashed back to her recent dinner with Josh. She'd told him everything he needed to know about the SX-2, from the general concept through the intricate workings of the system. Josh had gotten those out of her by asking detailed questions. Why hadn't she seen that his interest was excessive? Because she'd been too intent on impressing him, Valentina thought bitterly.

She recalled being a little uncomfortable afterward, but not really worried. Josh was Warren's self-proclaimed best

riend. Warren himself had discussed the project with him.
Not in such detail, though.

Valentina felt sick at the realization of what she'd done.
That was swiftly followed by white-hot anger. Josh had used
her, coldly and deliberately. He'd never cared about her. It
was all an act from the very beginning. No wonder he was
so unemotional when they said goodbye. He'd gotten everything he wanted.

Her eyes were glittering with blue fire as she dialed Josh's
number. She was prepared to do battle in case he refused to
talk to her, but his secretary put her through promptly.

"Hi, Valentina. What can I do for you?" He had the
nerve to sound completely normal.

"You've already done it," she answered furiously.

"I don't understand. What's wrong? Has something
happened to Warren? Did he have a relapse?"

"Warren is fine—or as good as he can be under the circumstances. Don't pretend you don't know what's wrong,"
she said scornfully.

"I *don't* know. Will you kindly tell me?"

"I intend to." Suddenly Valentina wanted to see his face
when she accused him, to make him look her in the eye and
try to explain his treachery. "Stay right where you are. I'll
be over in ten minutes." She hung up without giving him a
chance to reply.

Valentina had never been to Josh's office before. Warren
had told her he was very successful, but she didn't realize the
extent of his operation. The company occupied an entire,
sprawling two-story building built around an interior
courtyard complete with flowers, a fountain and outdoor
tables and chairs where the employees could have lunch.

Under ordinary circumstances Valentina would have been
impressed, but that day she was intent only on denouncing
Josh for his unforgivable behavior.

He didn't bother with preliminaries, evidently having decided to go on the offensive. "What the hell was that phone
call all about? I called Warren after you hung up on me, but
all I got was his voice mail."

"I'm not surprised," she answered with heavy sarcasm "He's a little busy right now with the police."

Josh stared at her blankly. "What are the police doin there?"

"Did you think he'd let you get away with it for old time' sake? You counted too heavily on friendship. What you di was a crime. I don't see how you could do a thing like tha to Warren, of all people!"

He took a deep breath. "Suppose you skip the recrimi nations and tell me what the devil you're talking about."

"Stop pretending you don't know that Draeger Softwar Systems came out this morning with a process identical t the SX-2."

His gaze sharpened. "I heard they had a blockbuster. I it the same kind of security system as Warren's?"

"It *is* his system. You should know, since you stole it!"

"You suspect *me?*" Josh stared at her incredulously.

"That was your plan all along, wasn't it, cozying up to m to get what you wanted. That's your specialty, isn't it Romancing women so they don't guess what you're reall after. You must have gotten a big laugh out of how easy was," she said bitterly. "I didn't even present you with challenge."

"I fail to see how our relationship has anything to do wit the theft of the SX-2."

"Oh, please! You expect me to believe you weren' pumping me for details that night we had dinner? Yo stopped just short of asking me to smuggle you the blue prints!"

"That's ridiculous! Naturally I was interested. It's a ver sophisticated concept."

"Just like you. It never entered my mind that you had th expertise to duplicate the process, once I outlined all th safeguards. Warren spent months perfecting that system and I handed it over to you in a couple of hours."

"You can't really believe I would rip him off," Josh sai slowly.

"How can you deny it?"

His expression hardened. "Perhaps you can explain why Draeger is marketing the product instead of my own company."

"Any moron could figure that out. If your name was on it, everyone would know you'd pirated the prototype. You're a regular visitor at Warren's offices."

"That's logical," he conceded. "I suppose I stole the idea and sold it to Draeger. Is that the scenario?"

"You undoubtedly were paid a fortune for it."

"Don't forget the fringe benefits," he drawled. "Their stock went up ten points. Anyone with inside information like that could have made a killing. Just enlighten me on one point. Why did I need the money?" He waved an arm around the spacious office. "I'm not in Warren's class, but I've done fairly well for myself."

"By taking chances, no doubt. Only they don't always work out. He tried to warn you that living on the edge was dangerous, but you wouldn't listen."

"Why should I, when I can get new capital so easily? Warren will never miss it. He has more money than he knows what to do with."

"Don't you have any scruples at all?"

In her secret heart, Valentina had hoped Josh would have some explanation, although she knew that was a futile wish. What possible excuse could there be for such a base betrayal? At the very least he could be remorseful, but he didn't even have the grace to look embarrassed.

"Friendship is one thing, business is another." He shrugged.

"You don't know the meaning of friendship," she flared. "You use people shamelessly and then throw them away!"

"I didn't take advantage of you as thoroughly as I might have." His eyes swept insolently over her taut body. "You were in a very generous mood the night you came to my apartment."

Color flooded her cheeks at the memory, but she faced him defiantly. "Don't try to take credit for the fact that nothing happened. You would have made love to me without any compunction. Too bad Cheryl spoiled your plans so

inconveniently. You could have found out what I knew a lo
sooner."

"At least you'd have gotten something in return," he sai
flippantly.

"Something I'd regret for the rest of my life!"

"Maybe not." He moved close enough to set her nerv
ends quivering. "You might have enjoyed yourself thor
oughly. That's the reason you came to my apartment, isn'
it? To find out what it would be like to lie naked in my arm
while I satisfied your passion."

"No! That isn't—I never wanted you to make love t
me."

His mouth curved in a sardonic smile. "You were mor
honest that night."

Every admission she'd made was burned into Valentina'
memory. To her eternal shame, she was still affected by th
nearness of his hard, lean-hipped body. He was taunting he
with his maleness, but at least now she realized the attrac
tion he held for her was merely sexual. How could she eve
have imagined she was in love with him?

"I don't have your vast experience," she said raggedly
"It was easy for you to confuse me."

"If it makes you feel better to tell yourself I seduced you
go right ahead. But we both know that isn't true. If eithe
of us used the other, you're the guilty party. You wanted on
last fling, and you figured I was available. Or was an on
going affair in your plans?" he asked grimly. "A lot of sto
len afternoons of passion behind Warren's back?"

"How could you even think such a thing?" Valentina
gasped. "I would never cheat on Warren—or anyone else
cared about. I detest men like you!"

"That wasn't the impression you gave—on more than on
occasion, I might add," he said mockingly.

"I didn't know you for what you really are."

"It wouldn't have made any difference." He hooked a
hand around her neck and pulled her so close that their lip
were only inches apart. "If I kissed you now, you'd melt i
my arms and let me take you right here."

"You're wrong." She braced her palms against his chest and lowered her head to prevent him from carrying out his threat.

He snaked an arm around her waist while he jerked her chin up so she'd have to look at him. "Shall we try it and find out?" His eyes glittered with an almost savage light.

Josh's close embrace was having its usual devastating effect, but Valentina refused to admit it. "Do you intend to add rape to your other crimes?" she asked through gritted teeth.

"I won't have to use force." His lips brushed hers in a feathery caress that made her legs feel weak. "We've always wanted each other." One hand skimmed her side, gliding tantalizingly close to the swelling curve of her breast. "Sometimes I think you were sent from hell to punish me for whatever sins I might have committed."

Every inch of her body was crying out for satisfaction. The full power of this man must be awesome. He could bring her more ecstasy than she'd ever known.

With a supreme effort of will, Valentina broke out of his embrace. "I hope they send you to prison for a long time," she said in an unsteady voice. "You're utterly without a conscience."

Her rapid breathing brought a smile of grim amusement to his hard face. "Would it make you more lenient if I were repentant?"

"Nothing could redeem you in my eyes!"

"Then I'll just have to console myself with my ill-gotten gains."

"How can you laugh about what you did?" she exclaimed. "I know you don't care about my opinion, but doesn't Warren's disillusionment mean anything to you?"

Josh's eyes were suddenly bleak. "People disappoint each other all the time. I think we've covered the subject. Go home, Valentina."

Valentina drove around aimlessly after leaving Josh. She had to compose herself before confessing to Warren what she'd done. Her own part in the wretched affair was bad enough, but at least it was inadvertent. He would really be crushed by Josh's perfidy. This was no time for Warren to guess that she had anything else to feel sorry about.

The cars were gone from the driveway when she returned to the house. That meant the detectives had completed their preliminary investigation, and the managers had gone back to the main office. Warren would have time to talk to her. Valentina knew she couldn't put it off, but her steps lagged as she went into the house.

Florence came out of his office, looking haggard. "I still can't believe it."

She was due for an even bigger shock, Valentina thought sadly, but she had to tell Warren first. "How's he taking it?"

"Better than the rest of us," Florence said.

That would change, when she shattered all his illusions. Valentina went into Warren's office and closed the door.

He always had a smile for her, even today. "It's good to see your pretty face after all the gloom and doom around here this morning. I suppose you heard what happened."

"Yes, Florence told me the bad news. I'm so terribly sorry."

"I blame myself in a way. I should have been more aware of what was going on."

"That's nonsense! You took every precaution."

"Except the one that would have prevented this tragedy." He sighed deeply. "Well, you're never too old to learn."

"Is there any way you can prove that Draeger was involved?"

"It will be difficult. Our attorneys are looking into the matter. From what I can tell, they made enough changes to claim their system is different. The alterations are minor, but they'll say they were working along parallel lines and simply came out with the product first."

"So there's nothing you can do?" she asked sadly.

"I didn't say that. It promises to be a long, nasty battle, but I believe we have a good chance of winning. Don't look so tragic, sweetheart." He smiled at her forlorn face. "It wasn't your fault."

"But that's just the point. It was."

Warren gave her a puzzled frown. "I don't understand."

"I never meant to do it. You have to believe that. It was sheer stupidity on my part. I simply never realized he was capable of such an underhanded act." Her words came tumbling out.

"Slow down. I don't know what you're talking about."

Valentina took a deep breath. "I was the one who told Josh how the SX-2 worked. I practically drew him a picture."

Warren seemed bewildered. "You don't know that much about electronics."

"But Josh does. I told him everything you told me about the project—the way the voice print works, how an alarm goes off when the system is being invaded. He hung on every word," she said with bitter irony.

"Of course he'd be interested. It's a breakthrough in security systems, but that doesn't—"

"How can you even think of defending him?" she broke in. "Don't you understand? The man you thought of as a son stole from you! And I helped him. That's the thing I'll never forgive myself for. I should have seen through him, even if you didn't."

"Val, dear, you mustn't—"

She interrupted him again. "Please don't be forgiving, Warren. Neither of us deserves it. Josh is a thief, and I'm a fool. It isn't as if I didn't know about men like him. They use people." She gazed at him through a blur of tears. "I'm only sorry I let you change my mind about him, instead of the other way around."

"I haven't been very astute about any of the people close to me," Warren said heavily.

"Join the club. I never trusted Josh, but I started to think I'd misjudged him when we spent that week in the country together. I didn't want to go, but you maneuvered me into it. Remember?"

"I remember," Warren answered without emotion.

"Not that it was your fault. Who could have imagined I was part of his long-range plans."

"Is that what you believe?"

"How can I doubt it? We didn't get along very well here at home, but he changed completely when we got up there. We really had a lot of fun that week, and he was so good with the youngsters. They were streetwise kids who could spot a phony in a minute, but he won their complete respect. That's what I don't understand. How could he be such a Jekyll and Hyde?" she asked helplessly.

"Josh didn't steal the SX-2," Warren said quietly.

"I know you don't want to believe it," she said sorrowfully. The poor man was in denial, but that couldn't last.

"It's true. Chuck sold the plans to Draeger."

"Chuck! That's almost harder to believe!"

"Not really. All the warning signs were there, if I'd bothered to notice. Denise was draining him dry with her demands for clothes and jewelry and expensive evenings out. He was exhausted, both physically and mentally."

"He *has* looked awfully haggard lately," Valentina said slowly, trying to absorb this new turn of events.

"Small wonder. Chuck simply couldn't afford the lifestyle Denise insisted on, but he was afraid she'd leave him if he didn't give her everything she asked for. He was facing bankruptcy and didn't know where to turn."

"He could have come to you for a loan."

"I'd already lent him money. He was ashamed to ask for more. Besides, that was no solution. Only a very rich man could satisfy Denise's requirements, and this was the only way Chuck could think of to get a sizable amount of cash."

"He must have been really desperate to do a thing like that. How did he expect to get away with it? Didn't he realize he'd be the first one the police would suspect?"

"Obviously he wasn't thinking clearly. He told some vague story about forgetting to lock the plans in the safe one night, but it would be an unlikely coincidence for a thief to pick the only night the plans were accessible."

"Anyway, he'd have to get in the house first," Valentina pointed out.

"Exactly. And we've had no signs of forced entry. When the detectives questioned him at length, Chuck broke down and confessed. It was very painful. He couldn't live with what he'd done."

"I'm not surprised. The SX-2 was his baby. He's been working on it for months."

"Yes, it's very sad to see a young man ruin a bright future in one impulsive moment." Warren sighed.

"What's going to happen to him? Will he have to go to prison?"

"That wouldn't serve any purpose. Chuck isn't a criminal in the ordinary sense of the word. He's simply a man who snapped under unbearable pressure. I don't intend to press charges."

"Not many men would look at it that way. He may have cost you a fortune."

Warren shrugged. "I have more money than I could spend in several lifetimes. I'm more concerned about what this will do to him."

"He'll have to find a new career. The electronics industry is all Chuck knows, but he won't be able to find a job when this gets out."

"That's undoubtedly true, so I'm going to ask Josh to take him on."

Valentina was abruptly jolted back to her own problems, but they were too horrendous to contemplate now. "Do you think he'll do it?"

"I think so. Josh is a compassionate man. Chuck will have to earn his trust, but I believe everything will work out in time."

"His basic problem isn't solved—unless Denise leaves him, which wouldn't surprise me. He'll have even less to offer her now."

"It would be the best thing that ever happened to him, but that isn't up to us to decide. For Chuck's sake, I've asked her to come here for a little talk." Warren looked uncharacteristically forbidding.

"Do you think it will do any good?" Valentina was obviously doubtful.

"I don't know, but it's time somebody told her the hard facts of life." Warren looked up as Florence stuck her head in the door. "Denise is here to see you."

"Tell her to wait." He stopped Valentina as she rose to leave. "You don't have to go."

"It might be less embarrassing if you had a private talk."

"I'm not concerned with her feelings," he said grimly. "Stay here, this won't take long. After I get through with Denise, I want to have a little talk with you, too."

She was vaguely disquieted. Was Warren going to lecture her after all about the imprudence of leaking information, even if it hadn't led to this disaster? Well, she certainly had it coming. Valentina sank back in her chair.

Chapter Eleven

Warren's expression was enigmatic as he gazed across the desk at Denise. She was expensively dressed in white silk pants and a brilliantly printed designer blouse. Several gold bangles adorned one wrist, and a costly gold watch with a lapis face decorated the other.

"I feel so awful about what happened," she said as soon as she sat down. "I don't know what prompted Chuck to do such a terrible thing."

"Don't you?" Warren asked evenly.

"Of course not! You don't think *I* was involved?" Denise looked startled.

"I believe you bear more of the responsibility than he does."

"Now just a damn minute! You're not going to hang this thing on *me*. Chuck will tell you I didn't know anything about it. If he said I did, he's lying!"

"He wouldn't turn on you if you were an ax murderess. Too bad you've never shown him the same loyalty," Warren said contemptuously.

"You have no right to say that! I've been a good wife to Chuck. If you don't believe me, ask him. He loves me."

"And do you love him?"

Her eyes slid away. "What kind of question is that? He' my husband. Of course I love him."

"Enough to stand by him now that he's out of a job?"

"He'll get another one."

"Not without my help—and not at the same salary he wa making. Are you prepared to scale down your standard o living?"

"It isn't all that grand now," she muttered.

"You'll look back on it as the lap of luxury," Warren sai curtly. "I want you to understand what the future holds There won't be any more designer clothes or evenings at ex pensive nightclubs. You'll have to stop demanding thing Chuck can't afford. Can you live with that?"

"It's none of your business," she answered sullenly.

"On the contrary, it's something I need to know. If I'n going to recommend Chuck for a job, I have to be sure yo won't goad him into doing something this foolish again."

"I don't know why you blame *me*. I didn't tell him to g out and commit a crime. Chuck wanted me to have nic things. How did I know he couldn't afford them?"

"I'm sure he tried to tell you, but you weren't intereste in where the money came from as long as you got every thing you wanted. Otherwise you pouted or threw a tan trum, probably even withheld sex," Warren surmise shrewdly. "It isn't surprising that Chuck finally snapped You sucked him dry, financially and emotionally."

"I don't have to listen to this." Denise rose to her feet.

"Sit down."

Warren didn't raise his voice. The force of his personal ity was enough. Her defiance crumbled and she slowly re sumed her seat.

"The question is, where do you go from here? You ca divorce Chuck." His tone was as dispassionate as if he wer discussing a business deal. "That would take a huge load of his back. But then what would you do? Don't count on bi alimony payments. If you're awarded anything, it will be pittance. Chuck won't be earning much."

"He'd want to take care of me," she said uncertainly.

"With what?" Warren asked bluntly. "You'd be bette off looking for another husband. You're an attractive woman. The only trouble is, there are a lot of younger, equally attractive women out there who are also looking for rich men. The chances of finding one who thinks you're a gift from heaven are slim.''

She stared at him in bewilderment. "I don't understand. Are you telling me to leave Chuck, or not to leave him?''

"That's up to you. I'm merely pointing out your options.''

"Why? You don't care what happens to me.''

"No, but I care about him. Chuck needs you right now—but as a wife, not a pampered pet. Either help him or get out of his life.''

"How could I be any help?''

"For starters, you could get a job.''

"I don't know how to do anything.''

"You must have done some kind of work in your lifetime.''

"I worked in a department store after I graduated from high school,'' she said slowly. "I started in junior sportswear, but after a couple of months they put me in the designer dress department.''

"You showed an aptitude for fashion even then,'' Warren commented dryly.

"I've always liked beautiful clothes. Is that a crime? I was a better salesgirl than any of the older women who'd been there for years,'' she said defiantly.

"I don't doubt it for a moment. You might have been a huge success if you'd pursued a career in fashion. Most buyers start as saleswomen. The really knowledgeable ones go to the couturier shows in Paris and Rome.''

Denise's eyes were wistful. "Imagine getting paid to do that.''

"You could be one of the select group. Success wouldn't come overnight, but if you stuck to it, I'll bet you'd achieve your goal. You certainly have the drive to get what you want,'' he couldn't help adding.

"I haven't worked in years,'' she said tentatively. "Do you think anyone would hire me?''

"I doubt if you'd have any trouble getting a sales job, but if you do, give me a call. The manager of Champlain's is a friend of mine." He named an exclusive local department store.

Denise gazed at him with mixed emotions. "I know you're doing this for Chuck's sake, even though it's against your better judgment. Maybe I haven't been the best wife in the world, but whether you believe it or not, I never dreamed he'd do what he did."

"I believe you. He should have been honest about what he could and couldn't afford. That was his mistake."

"Sure, I wanted to live like you do. Who wouldn't? But it was more than that. You were all so confident, you and Val and Josh." She turned to acknowledge Valentina's presence for the first time. "I wanted to be part of your inner circle, to be accepted. I haven't made many friends since I moved up here," Denise said regretfully.

Valentina suffered a pang of conscience, remembering her constant rejection of the other woman. "Maybe you pushed a little too hard," she said uncomfortably.

"It's the only way I know how. Nothing was ever handed to me. I've had to work hard for everything I wanted—not that it's ever done me much good."

"How can you say that? You have a husband who adores you. A lot of women would consider themselves lucky to be in your shoes."

"Being ambitious isn't a bad thing," Warren said. "You just have to channel your energies into something more constructive than social position. Whether you stay with Chuck or not, take my advice and go to work. You'll find it a lot more rewarding than depending on material things to make you happy."

"I think I'm going to give it a try." She flashed him a gamine smile. "What choice do I have? Hollywood isn't exactly breaking down my door."

"Forget the movies," Valentina said. "Go to work at Champlain's. I'll be your first customer."

"You didn't want to have anything to do with me before," Denise said pointedly. "Why did I suddenly get more acceptable?"

"We never had anything in common before, but I have hopes for the future." Valentina smiled.

"Strangely enough, I do, too." Denise stood and looked at Warren. "I suppose I should say thank you, but I'm not that rehabilitated yet. You said some rotten things to me."

He stood, also, and held out his hand. "I hope they helped. Good luck, Denise."

After she left, Valentina said, "She has a lot more intelligence than we gave her credit for. Who would ever have suspected?"

"I'm afraid we shouldn't have dismissed her so automatically. That's one more thing I have to feel sorry about."

"You've made up for it by trying to straighten them both out. That was an inspired suggestion of yours. Denise is really savvy about clothes. She'd make a fabulous buyer."

"Especially since she already has so much experience at it," Warren said ironically.

Valentina grinned. "And this time Chuck wouldn't have to pay the bills." Her face sobered. "Do you think she'll stick by him?"

"It's entirely possible. Denise knows she won't find that kind of devotion too readily—if at all. I just hope Chuck will show a little backbone for a change. He needs to stand up to her once in a while for their marriage to work."

"I don't know if he can change that much. He's always been so afraid of losing her that it clouded his judgment."

Warren gazed at her with an unreadable expression. "Love has been known to do that to people."

"You can't allow it to destroy you."

"Denying it can be just as destructive."

She looked puzzled. "That's one thing Chuck was never guilty of."

"I was talking about you. How long are you and Josh going to pretend you're not in love?" Warren asked quietly.

Valentina paled. "How can you even suggest such a thing?"

"I've suspected it for a long time, but I thought perhaps it was all in my mind. Today, I knew for sure that it wasn't. Your anguish when you thought Josh had stolen the SX-2 was very revealing."

"Naturally I was upset," she said defensively. "I know how you feel about him. You would have been devastated."

"Not as badly as you were," he said dryly. "Only a woman in love would react that strongly to the idea of being used."

"How did you expect me to feel? I thought I'd handed him your secret project."

"Josh is good, but he couldn't have reproduced the plans from your conversation alone."

"He asked me explicit questions," she insisted. "Especially about the defense system, and what methods it used. Why else would he want information like that?"

"It was purely professional interest. Given the time and the inclination, he might have developed something similar, but certainly not by a description alone. It's an impossibility, given the complexities of the program."

"I didn't realize that," Valentina said slowly.

"Josh must have been very angry at your suspicions. Did you argue?"

She lowered her head at the memory of his cold eyes and the cutting things he said. "That part doesn't matter. We've never gotten along very well. I'm just glad I was wrong about him."

"Josh is justifiably proud of his integrity. You're going to have a devil of a time making it up to him."

"I'll apologize of course, but I don't expect it will do any good. We both said too many hurtful things."

Warren smiled unexpectedly. "It's at times like these that I wouldn't care to be young again. I don't have the energy for those impassioned lovers' quarrels."

"Josh and I were never lovers!"

"You don't have to tell me that, honey. I know neither of you would ever do anything behind my back. I only wish you'd come to me when you realized how you felt about Josh." He held up a hand as she started to speak. "It's obvious when you're together. The electricity fairly crackles between you."

"That's because we disagree on practically everything."

"You argue because you're both decent people and you don't want to hurt me. That's admirable, but it doesn't make the problem go away. You can't stop loving someone because it's inconvenient."

"How can I convince you that you're wrong? I'll admit I find him somewhat attractive," Valentina said carefully. "Josh went out of his way to be charming for your sake, and I was friendly for the same reason. We knew you wanted us to like each other."

"Throwing you together was another example of my remarkable naïveté." Warren sighed. "Naturally sparks would ignite. You're both extremely attractive, and you have everything in common—like youth."

"You're not going to bring up that age thing again! We agreed it was unimportant."

"I was only kidding myself," he said sadly. "I can't give you the leaping excitement Josh can. I still remember what it was like. I had that with Marian. You deserve to have it, too."

"What you and I have together is very satisfying," Valentina said earnestly.

"You shouldn't settle for middle-aged pleasures, my dear. Not at your age. You and Josh belong together."

She shook her head. "He isn't in love with me," she said in a muffled voice.

"Is that why his eyes follow you constantly, and even the most casual contact turns you both into living statues? That last Sunday at the pool was most revealing."

Valentina chose her words with great care. "Perhaps there is some physical attraction between us. It's normal to respond to the opposite sex occasionally. I've noticed you eyeing pretty women. It doesn't mean anything."

"Don't underestimate sex, my dear. It's a very powerful force. But you and Josh are completely compatible in every other way, too. I saw you both come alive when you were reminiscing about your experiences at camp. You two have everything going for you except the freedom to declare your love, and I'm giving you my permission. Don't look so tragic, honey." Warren cupped her cheek in his palm lovingly. "I'll be all right."

"I'm so sorry," she whispered, since it was futile to keep on denying what was so glaringly evident. "I've let you down terribly."

"You mustn't feel that way. I'm as concerned about your happiness as you are about mine. We'll still be a family." A mischievous smile lit up his face. "I've always looked on Josh as a son. Now I'll have a daughter to worry over, too."

Valentina didn't want to dash his expectations for herself and Josh, so she smiled mistily. "I hope you'll continue to let me share your life."

"I insist on it, but you're not to feel responsible for me. It's time I stopped leaning on you two and developed my own resources."

"We haven't felt you were an obligation," she protested. "I don't want you to be lonely, just because you think you're imposing."

"I won't be alone. Florence will keep me company," he joked, then his expression turned thoughtful. "It's strange that I've worked with her all these years without realizing what a delightful woman she is."

That was the only thing that made Valentina feel any better. Florence would make Warren happy if he gave her the chance—and the odds were good that something would develop between them.

Valentina drove home, trying to think positively. Florence's dreams had a chance of coming true, Chuck's career wasn't destroyed irrevocably, and Denise was pointed in the right direction. Only her own life was in ruins. She'd lost both men. If there was ever a chance for a relationship with Josh, it was gone now.

He would never forgive her for accusing him so unjustly. She cringed at the memory of the contemptuous words they'd flung at each other. The last thing she wanted was to go through another such scene, but Valentina knew she had to apologize. Josh had a right to get even.

Without giving herself a chance to think about it, Valentina went directly to the phone when she reached her apartment. But after psyching herself up for the confrontation, she couldn't reach him.

"Mr. Derringer is in a meeting," his secretary told her. "May I take a message?"

"No, I'll try again," Valentina said tonelessly. She was afraid he wouldn't call her back.

When she phoned a little later, the woman said, "I'm sorry, but he's out of the office, and I don't know when he'll return."

It was torture to have to wait until evening when she could reach him at home, but Valentina had no choice. It promised to be a long afternoon.

She started telephoning Josh's apartment from five o'clock on, but he never came home. All she got was his answering machine. He must have gone out right from work.

Valentina was faced with the prospect of having to wait until the next day to track him down—with possibly the same lack of success, which was insupportable. She couldn't continue to have this hanging over her head.

There was only one thing to do. She would have to go over to his apartment house and wait in the lobby until he returned. It could prove embarrassing. Josh might bring somebody home with him. Valentina wavered, then set her chin. He'd just have to spare her a few moments. What she had to say wouldn't take long, and maybe the presence of a third party would shorten his recriminations.

"I'm going to wait in the lobby for Mr. Derringer," Valentina told the doorman on duty.

"I'll buzz him and tell him you're here," the man said.

"Did he come home?" Her heart sank.

If she'd only been a little more patient she could have avoided a face-to-face confrontation. Whereas last time she'd welcomed it, this time she didn't. But it was too late now.

"I've changed my mind. I'll go up. I know the apartment number." She walked swiftly to the elevator before the man could stop her.

Josh was standing in his doorway when she got off at his floor. The doorman had obviously alerted him. He looked even less welcoming than last time.

"What are you doing here?" he asked curtly.

"I want to talk to you for a few minutes."

"Is there something you forgot to accuse me of? The drug problem? The plight of the homeless?"

"May I come in?" she asked quietly. "I promise I won't stay long."

He stood aside grudgingly and led the way to the den. When they got there he didn't ask her to sit down. Josh wasn't going to make this easy for her.

Valentina moistened her lips nervously. "I came to apologize."

"For what? You accused me of so many things," he drawled. "Which one did you decide I'm not guilty of?"

"You have every right to be angry. I should have known you'd never steal from Warren."

"Well, at least I'm absolved of one crime. How about seduction? Am I in the clear on that, too?"

She didn't want to discuss anything personal. "I shouldn't have jumped to conclusions, but you didn't even try to set me straight. You could have told me it wasn't possible to reconstruct the plans from a description alone."

"How did you find out—from Warren?" Josh's grim face relaxed for the first time. "You have a lot to learn about electronics."

"Why didn't you tell me that, instead of pretending you were completely unprincipled?"

His expression hardened again. "It was what you wanted to hear."

"That's not true! I was devastated."

"Only because you thought I used you to get the information."

She looked away. "Naturally I was upset to think I was responsible."

"Was that the real reason, Valentina?" he asked softly. "Or did it make you furious to think I used you the way you tried to use me?"

"How did I ever try to use *you?*" she asked incredulously.

"Don't tell me you didn't come to my apartment that night with the intention of making love. Your interest in me has always and only been sexual." Josh's face was set in

stern lines. "I might have been flattered under different circumstances, but Warren is my friend. I can't forgive you for
provoking me into several incidents I'm ashamed of."

"Don't you think I was, too?"

"That's hard to believe. The night of the awards dinner
we agreed to stay away from each other. Then a couple of
hours later you showed up at my place. What explanation
do you have for that?"

Her long lashes swept down. "It was an error in judgment. I thought we had something to talk about, but I realized I was wrong."

"Only after Cheryl came in with her key. Before that you
said you were having doubts about your marriage. Was that
another of your little tricks?"

"No, it was true," she murmured.

He looked at her searchingly. "But you didn't break off
the engagement."

"I . . . well, I reconsidered."

"That's a convenient explanation." Josh smiled sardonically. "What a sucker I am! You almost had me believing
you again. Fun and games are one thing, but you aren't
about to let Warren slip through your fingers."

"I'm not going to marry him," Valentina said quietly.

"How many times do you think you can pull the same
trick?" he asked roughly. "And what makes you think I
give a damn?"

"I know you don't. I just wanted to set the record
straight."

"Does Warren know about this?"

"Yes, we had a long talk today."

"I would have thought he'd have other things on his
mind, with the theft and all. How did it happen to come up
today?"

"I was quite upset when I came back from talking to you.
I'm afraid I said some rather harsh things about the way you
used people for your own purposes. Somehow or other
Warren got the impression that you and I . . ." Her voice
trailed off.

Josh's eyes narrowed. "I'm beginning to get the picture.
You didn't break the engagement, Warren did."

"It was by mutual agreement."

"Don't hand me that! He's always been perceptive about people. Warren could tell we were attracted to each other. But how the hell could you let him think it was anything more than that?"

"I didn't! I told him we hadn't done anything wrong."

"I'm sure you tried, anyway," Josh said grimly. "Too bad he didn't believe you. Which means he thinks *I* was sneaking around behind his back, too."

"You're wrong. Warren knows neither of us would do that to him."

"If that's true, why did he call off the wedding?"

Valentina's hands were clasped so tightly that her knuckles were white. "He got the mistaken impression that you and I are in love with each other."

"That's a laugh!" Josh smiled mirthlessly.

"I told him so, but he thought I was only trying to spare his feelings. He said we shouldn't be concerned about him, our happiness was the important thing. I did my best to convince him that he's wrong about us, but his mind was made up."

Josh was staring at her speculatively. "Now I'm beginning to get it. You didn't come here to apologize, you came to latch onto another meal ticket. I'm not as wealthy as Warren, but you blew that one, so you're prepared to lower your sights." He looked her over insolently. "I'm sorry to disappoint you, but marriage isn't in my plans. I might be willing to satisfy your needs in some other way, though."

Anger penetrated Valentina's misery. "Don't flatter yourself! I wouldn't let you touch me if my life depended on it."

"We've disproved that point on numerous occasions," he answered mockingly. "I'm beginning to think you say provocative things like that on purpose."

"You're wrong, but I'm not interested in arguing with you—it would be a waste of time. Your ego is too colossal. I'm familiar with men like you," she said bitterly. "You think you're God's gift to women. Actually you're proof that He has a sense of humor."

"So we're back to men bashing," Josh taunted. "I've always wondered what one of us did to arouse such ire. Since we'll probably never see each other again, why don't you enlighten me?"

"You'd love to find out some other man succeeded in humiliating me, wouldn't you?"

"On the contrary." His mocking expression changed as he stared at her flushed cheeks. "I'd like to know what made you so afraid of love."

"I don't believe in love—at least not between a man and a woman. It's a word men use to get what they want."

"I'm sorry somebody hurt you so badly," he said slowly.

"Don't be. I recovered."

"That's debatable. Your wounds still aren't healed."

"That's what you'd like to think," she scoffed.

"Do you really believe I hate you that much?"

"It doesn't matter anymore." The fire suddenly left her. "You've always misjudged me. What's one more instance?"

"Is that what you want me to think, that you're callous and calculating, incapable of any tender feelings?"

"You always have," she replied simply. "We've never gotten along."

"I could cite some notable examples to refute that."

"You're referring to sex again. All right, I'll admit I was attracted to you. Is that what you want to hear?"

"I want to know what he did to you," Josh said quietly. "Not to gloat. Only to help you start the healing process. What if you overreacted all this time? Maybe you just misunderstood something he said or did."

"That's really very funny. Okay, you won't be satisfied until you find out, so here goes." Valentina took a deep breath. "I was in love with a man once—someone a lot like you. He wasn't as rich or as polished, but he was very handsome, and quite irresistible to women. I was flattered when he was attracted to me. I fell in love with him almost instantly."

"Are you sure it was love and not merely infatuation?"

"I was convinced it was love. He was everything I'd ever dreamed of. I was young and I'd never really been in love before." She paused, recalling that long-ago passion.

When she didn't continue, Josh said, "I didn't mean to interrupt. Go on."

"I had great plans," she said in an unemotional voice, as though speaking of someone else. "After Robert told me he loved me, I thought the next step would be marriage. When he didn't mention it, I dropped hints and dragged him to visit happy couples in the suburbs. He wasn't impressed, but I thought it was just a bachelor's natural skittishness about losing his freedom. I didn't realize he truly didn't want to marry me."

"The man was a fool," Josh muttered under his breath, but Valentina was too engrossed in painful memories to hear.

"When it finally sank in, I knew I couldn't go on the way we were. Sooner or later he'd meet someone else, and the longer I stayed with him, the harder it would be to let go. I told him it was over and I didn't intend to see him anymore."

"But he didn't want to lose you completely, so he proposed," Josh said ironically.

"Bingo," she replied with equal irony. "You'd think I'd have been smart enough to figure out he was only stringing me along, but when you're on cloud nine, you don't expect to fall off."

"Obviously he backed out. I can understand why you were hurt, but you can't let one bad experience rule out any future relationships. There are guys like that in the world. You were just unlucky enough to get tangled up with a jerk."

"Wait, you haven't heard the whole story. When you and I first met, you kept trying to find out about my past life," she said in an apparent digression.

"It seemed a little strange that you were so secretive about it. You even shied away from discussing generalities, like whether your family lives in New York."

"I wasn't born there, as I told you. I come from a small town in central California, not far from here. I said I was a native New Yorker so you wouldn't decide to take a trip to Middlefield and ask a lot of questions about me."

He looked at her in bewilderment. "What would I have found out?"

Valentina forced herself to continue. "I wanted a big wedding with all my friends and family there. We know half the people in town. I had invitations printed and ordered a beautiful wedding gown. I planned to have six brides-maids, a flower girl and a ring bearer—the works."

"Don't tell me—!"

She cut off his exclamation, anxious now to get the story over with. "I went home two weeks before the wedding to make all the final arrangements. I called Robert every night to tell him about all the elaborate plans."

"You called *him,* he didn't ever call you?"

"You're a lot more astute than I was," she said wryly. "His lack of ardor didn't register, either. He always said he loved me—after I said it first. I should have gotten a clue when he kept making excuses for not coming to Middle-field a few days early as we agreed. A lot of my friends had parties planned for us, but Robert said he had to clear away all of his work first."

"What business was he in?"

"He's an insurance agent with a large company." Valen-tina brushed the hair off her forehead wearily. "There's no point in dragging this out. You've already guessed the end-ing. He never showed up. The church was filled with my family and friends—everybody but Robert. There was a comic song written once about a bride left waiting at the al-tar. You can take it from me, it's no joke."

Josh swore pungently. "That miserable creep! How could you fall for a guy like that?"

"I don't have very good judgment when it comes to men," she said forlornly.

"How many have you let get close to you?"

"Only a masochist makes the same mistake twice. Rob-ert said he loved me and I believed him. How could I ever trust my own judgment again?"

"You had a miserable experience. He took away your dignity and disillusioned you. Don't let him do any more damage. Don't let him make you afraid to love again."

"You're very compassionate, considering the way I misjudged you today."

"Our entire relationship has been a series of misunderstandings," Josh said somberly. "Every time we started to make a breakthrough, something happened to turn us into adversaries again. Like the incident with Cheryl. You never did tell me why you came to my apartment that night."

"It was another miscalculation on my part."

"I'd really like to know."

Valentina sighed deeply. "Why not? Maybe you'll finally understand why I never intend to get involved again. After we had that talk at the awards dinner, I got the impression that you . . . that maybe your feelings for me were more than just physical."

Josh's face was expressionless. "So you decided to use me to get even for what Robert had done to you."

"No! That wasn't it at all."

"Come on, Valentina, we're letting it all hang out. Why not admit you wanted to make me suffer the way you had. It would have been a fitting revenge, since the only interest you've ever had in me was sexual."

"I wish that's all it was," she said in a low voice. Josh was right, they might as well be honest with each other and end the relationship cleanly. She couldn't leave him with that impression of her. "I fell in love with you. If there was a chance that you felt the same way, I had to take it. When will I stop looking for signs that aren't there?" she asked despairingly. "I should have known better than to make the same mistake twice."

He gripped her shoulders hard. "Are you telling me the truth?"

"I've always been honest with you, even though you never believe me." She gazed at his strong face, memorizing every feature, although she would never forget a single thing about him.

Josh gathered her in his arms, holding her against his taut body. "Darling Valentina, we've made each other miserable for no good reason. Couldn't you tell how I felt about you? I've been in love with you for such a long time."

This close embrace was something she'd never expected to experience again. Valentina wanted to clasp her arms around his neck and allow herself to believe in miracles. She drew back reluctantly.

"You're a very kind person, Josh, but don't make the same mistake I did. I can see now that what I felt for Robert wasn't love."

"Do you really believe I'm confusing love with desire?" He framed her face in his palms and gazed at her tenderly. "You still have a lot to learn about men, angel, and I'm going to enjoy teaching you. It's been a long bumpy road, but you're mine now, and I'll never let you go."

"I wish I could believe that," she answered wistfully.

He laughed out of pure exultation as he lifted her in his arms and carried her over to the couch. "Maybe this will convince you."

When they were lying closely together, there was no doubt about his need. Josh's torrid kiss was as urgent as the hard body pressed against hers. While he probed her mouth deeply, his hands caressed her back, gliding down to cup her bottom and press her more tightly against the juncture of his thighs.

Valentina uttered a tiny cry of pleasure when his hand cupped her breast and his fingers circled her nipple erotically. The sensation was so arousing that she turned liquid with desire.

Her responsiveness delighted Josh. He groaned with happiness, lifting his head to stare at her with blazing eyes. "Tell me you're mine," he demanded.

"Completely," she answered softly.

"I won't feel secure until I'm certain of that. Tomorrow morning we're going down to City Hall and getting married."

She looked at him with incredulous joy. "Do you really mean it?"

"I've never had any doubts," he said gently. "This ceremony will be just for you and me. We'll have the big wedding you wanted, back in Middlefield, but I'm not taking any chance of something coming between us before then. Is that all right with you, my love?"

"What could be more perfect?" Valentina's eyes were like twin stars. "We'll have two anniversaries to celebrate each year."

"Every day will be a celebration as long as I'm with you," Josh said, lowering his head to kiss her with great tenderness.

*　*　*　*　*